G R JORDAN

The Man Everyone Wanted

A Kirsten Stewart Thriller

First edition

ISBN: 978-1-914073-97-7

This book was professionally typeset on Reedsy.
Find out more at reedsy.com

Every next level of your life will demand a different you.

LEONARDO DICAPRIO

Contents

Foreword

This novel is set around the highlands and islands of Scotland and while using the area and its people as an inspiration, the specific places and persons in this book are entirely fictitious. And I seriously hope that this kind of thing isn't going on in the highlands today!

Acknowledgement

To Ken, Jessica, Jean, Colin, Susan and Rosemary for your work in bringing this novel to completion, your time and effort is deeply appreciated.

Novels by G R Jordan

The Highlands and Islands Detective series (Crime)

1. Water's Edge
2. The Bothy
3. The Horror Weekend
4. The Small Ferry
5. Dead at Third Man
6. The Pirate Club
7. A Personal Agenda
8. A Just Punishment
9. The Numerous Deaths of Santa Claus
10. Our Gated Community
11. The Satchel
12. Culhwch Alpha
13. Fair Market Value
14. The Coach Bomber
15. The Culling at Singing Sands
16. Where Justice Fails
17. The Cortado Club
18. Cleared to Die
19. Man Overboard!
20. Antisocial Behaviour

Kirsten Stewart Thrillers (Thriller)

1. A Shot at Democracy
2. The Hunted Child
3. The Express Wishes of Mr MacIver
4. The Nationalist Express
5. The Hunt for 'Red Anna'
6. The Execution of Celebrity
7. The Man Everyone Wanted
8. Busman's Holiday

The Contessa Munroe Mysteries (Cozy Mystery)

1. Corpse Reviver
2. Frostbite
3. Cobra's Fang

The Patrick Smythe Series (Crime)

1. The Disappearance of Russell Hadleigh
2. The Graves of Calgary Bay
3. The Fairy Pools Gathering

Austerley & Kirkgordon Series (Fantasy)

1. Crescendo!
2. The Darkness at Dillingham
3. Dagon's Revenge

Chapter 01

S ally Grayson was approaching retirement and today, she looked with disdain around the shopping centre in the middle of Inverness. A child had been sick all over the carpeted floor, one of the very few carpeted areas within the shopping centre, at least outside of the shops. Sally had been sitting quite happily, enjoying a cup of tea and some moments rest, when the call had gone out for the cleaner. She had arrived and looked at the meaty chunks lying on the floor and a rather apologetic parent standing some feet away from them. The child, however, was now running around and Sally had wondered how they always managed to do that. One minute, they lose everything. The next, fit as a fiddle.

She'd taken the mop out, along with her bucket, and cleaned the floor with it, but only once she had picked up most of the solid form and deposited it in her bin. She was using those large rolls of blue paper that she seemed to get through so much of during her career. Little yellow signs had been placed around the area as she cleaned. She saw the people watching, looking at her, unsure if they were feeling for her or just simply disgusted at the mess.

From the windows of a coffee shop, she saw people look over

distastefully as if somehow, she'd been involved in ruining their beverages. There was a piece of cheesecake on one of the tables and she felt she might pop in when she'd finished her shift and have some. It had appeared some weeks ago, a new line that the cafe had taken in, and she'd tasted it once. It was by no means cheap, but it had been nice.

Sally finished up the last of her mopping, gave the area a good stare, and decided to leave the wet floor signs out for the meantime. She'd come back in an hour and pick them up because it wouldn't take long before the area was dry once again. As she started to push her trolley, she noticed a man standing in jeans and a jacket, but with sunglasses on, glancing left and right.

Normally, it wouldn't bother her, but he didn't have the gait of a shopper or even that annoyed, frustrated look of a husband or partner waiting for his better half to finish purchasing within a shop. Some men, she had noticed, would stand and fidget at doors jumping from side to side on a foot as if they were unable to control the frustration they felt. Others just plonked themselves down on the chairs, bums on a seat, in the middle of the main thoroughfare. They pulled out phones these days, gazing at them, and every now and again, staring back at the shop that was taking away their partner.

This man was different. He was looking for somebody. Sally passed by in front of him, stared straight at him, and yet the man didn't offer any rebuke. He simply kept up his watch, up and down the full length of the thoroughfare.

There was a large ark, a clock feature, up high in the centre. The clock began to strike, and Sally could see a number of kids gathered round watching it, their parents behind them eagerly looking at watches and wondering if they had time to do this. Back in its day, the clock had been such a wondrous feature, one at which significant crowds would gather, but these days, the colours looked somewhat jaded. Usually, it was the youngest of children that were still taken in by it. Various animals would appear and then disappear, causing delight to the youngest of faces. There was a time when Sally had been delighted to watch the kids smile and laugh, but everything these days just seem tired.

That man is still there, thought Sally, looking at him. She followed his gaze to see a similarly dressed man standing in the doorway of a clothes shop. *He'd just given a nod.* She was going to push her trolley of cleaning equipment through the crowd and back to her little cubbyhole where she hid out. Instead, because of a couple of dancing kids in front of her, she stopped. The clock only lasted a couple of minutes; she could wait. She didn't look up at it, but instead gazed back to the man outside the clothing store. He was looking back down the thoroughfare and she saw a woman looking back at him. Was there some sort of signal given there? The woman's hand had moved. A number of fingers had been quickly put out and put back in again.

The thing about being the cleaning lady was that no one really noticed you. No one really looked, but you could notice people. You spotted when people were shoppers, when people were just dragged along, or when someone was simply cutting through, staying out of the rain, or maybe sprinting off for that sandwich that the stores provided. There were all sorts of people that passed through here, all looking at different things, all wanting something, but rarely did you see anyone standing and communicating from doorways. She could have gone over, asked them what they were doing, but in truth, she didn't care. Two weeks and Sally was out of here. Two weeks and she'd be getting on that bus for the airport. Málaga. Málaga would be the start of her retirement and there was no way Sally was letting herself get dragged into some shenanigans before she went.

A man pushed through in front of the kids, knocking one child on his backside as he strode. Sally was indignant and about to step forward and have a word, when she saw the man at the clothes store suddenly react. He took off into a run and from out of his pocket, she saw him pull a gun.

The man who had barged through was suddenly thrown as several shots hit his body. Sally screamed as the blood went everywhere and quickly tried to get behind her cleaning trolley. In front of her, the kid on the floor was crying loudly and she could see his face splattered with some of the blood from the man who had been shot. Sally crawled forward, putting herself over the child, but her ears began to ring as more shots were fired.

Sally felt a hand grab her on the shoulder and she turned her head to look into the face of a distraught woman who reached forward for her child. Sally could see a pram behind her, but the woman was dressed in high heels, a short skirt, and some sort of fur jacket. In the midst of all the terror that was going on, all her brain could think was, *Why did you dress like that to bring the kids out?* Another shot brought her back to reality and Sally let the woman grab the child, pulling the wee one onto their feet. She heard the clip of her heels as the woman ran, pushing the pram in front of her.

Sally saw an elderly man starting to shake on his seat in the middle of the thoroughfare. It looked like he was having some sort of a heart attack because he was clutching at his chest. She looked up to see if she could reach him but in the middle of the thoroughfare, there was a firefight, guns unloading their deadly packages from here and there. She saw the woman the man had been looking at pitch up against the window of a shop before gunfire shattered it and she fell through. Sally tried to crawl forward to the man who was having the heart attack, but as she got close, he was hit in the crossfire and fell off the chair in front of her, his face landing in front of hers. His eyes were dead, simply staring forward.

Sally tried to roll away, but someone ran past her and their foot caught her shoulder, sending them tumbling to the floor. She winced at the pain of the kick. As she looked up, she saw it was a gunman and he stood up, pointing the gun at her before realising she was just a bystander. She prayed aloud, begging him not to shoot. For a moment, she thought her prayers had been answered. The gun then fell from his hands. His body pitched forward. Sally looked up into the face of a man holding a bloody knife. He didn't wait to confront her, but neither was he concerned that she would identify him. Instead, he turned on his heel and ran.

It was less than three minutes from when the shooting had started, and Sally thought it had reached a low. She stared down the thoroughfare, saw the glass from the shattered windows where bullets had penetrated. She counted at least five bodies lying on the ground. Who knew if there were any more? Slowly, she crawled back to her cart, got up to her feet, but remained crouched behind it.

Sally stayed there for the next five minutes, her body shaking, her mind racing with images, until a security guard took her by the arm, telling her it was all right, and leading her into one of the shops. A few moments after she entered, the metal shutter was put down in front of it. She found herself in a crowd of people, all looking at each other in fear and terror. A man was telling them all to sit down on the ground, stay quiet until they could be assured that the place was safe again. Sally saw the old man's face, the one who had died in front of her. The hell with two weeks, she was out of here. She'd never come back to this place.

Scene break, scene break, scene break.

Detective Sergeant Hope McGrath stood at the far end of the thoroughfare looking at the scene in front of her. Paramedics had cleared away after doing what they could for the people in front of them. The forensic team had arrived and marked out where the bodies had been and had little yellow markers indicating where spent bullets were lying or where other important details were to be found.

Hope worked in the murder investigation team based in Inverness and was waiting for the arrival of her boss who had been at a conference and who was called back rather abruptly. While she awaited his arrival, Hope had been detailing who the witnesses were, making sure they were getting medical attention, but at the same time, were also getting processed to find out what they knew. It was a fine balance with some of them for they were a mess and details could be lost so easily. She had to brief teams of uniform police and make sure the entire area was secure, while organizing places for quick interviews to happen. Having done all that, she now stood at the end of the thoroughfare looking at the scene of devastation in front of her.

She shopped here. She had bought clothes in some of these

shops, food in other places. This was part of her life that had been ripped apart. In many ways, she was beginning to struggle with the scene of devastation.

'McGrath, what on earth? Do we have any idea?'

'Seoras,' said Hope. Looking over at her boss, Detective Inspector Seoras Macleod, a man she had worked with for many years, and with whom she had seen many devastating incidents.

'It's reminding me of Neptune's Staircase, Seoras,' said Hope. 'This is brutal, except . . .'

'What?' asked Macleod.

'I think it's more clinical. I was talking to Jona, and she said that some of these shots to take people out, they were good, very good. Not some random punter. Also seem to be shots coming from here, there, and everywhere. It's not a lone gunman. The weapons used, they'd be used by professionals.'

'Have we seen anything of Kirsten?' asked Macleod. He meant Kirsten Stewart who'd worked with him as a detective constable but who was now working for the secret services within the UK, mainly in the Inverness area. With what had just happened, Macleod was fully expecting her to be on scene. He walked over to a small table where he found some covers for his shoes. He put on a white coverall suit as well, indicated Hope should join him, and walked his way through the carnage outside a coffee shop.

He saw some little plastic signs advising there was a wet floor and he tried to weigh up the scene of what had happened. Glancing up, he saw the clock that had been part of the thoroughfare for years and noticed that two of the animals had shot marks. He bent down, looking at the outline of a male figure close to the bench in the middle of the thoroughfare.

There was still blood on the floor around it. Macleod glanced round at the smashed glass fronting several stores.

'Carnage,' he said. 'Just carnage.'

'No, Seoras,' said Hope. 'There's method here. They were after somebody. Something's not right. Jona talked about crossfire, two sides. She's trying to pull it together, but—'

'CCTV here?'

'A lot of the shops, but not here. We'll be going through it.'

Macleod went down to his knees again, followed by Hope. 'This is murder,' he said, 'but it's also something more.'

'Very perceptive, Inspector.'

Macleod rose and turned to look at a woman behind them dressed in a white coverall suit, but still managed to have a thorough and professional look about her.

'Miss Hunt,' said Macleod, 'this must be serious if you're actually here.'

'It's very serious, Inspector, but I'm afraid I can't talk to you about that, can I? We'll be taking it from here. Thank you and your team for your efforts. I'll talk to Miss Nakamura about where I want the forensic report sent. Some of our own people will be here soon enough.'

'This is a shopping centre,' said Macleod, 'a firefight in a shopping centre. You're meant to prevent this.'

'I'm well aware of that, Inspector,' said Hunt. 'As soon as we find these people, we'll close down on it, but I obviously can't comment on operational matters.'

'I was expecting to see our friend,' said Macleod. 'Is she okay?'

'She's fine,' said Anna Hunt, referring to Kirsten Stewart. 'She's on a slight leave of absence at the moment.'

'Nothing wrong, I hope?' queried Hope.

'Again, something I can't comment on,' said Anna Hunt, stepping past Macleod, looking at the blood on the floor. Her face didn't seem to show the same horror that had come across Macleod's. 'However, I think she could be back to work soon,' said Anna. With that, she turned around and held out her hand. 'Thank you, Inspector, but I'll take it from here.' Macleod reached forward, gave her hand a firm shake.

'Just make sure the paperwork is over with me.'

'Of course. Now if you don't mind.'

Macleod felt he'd been dismissed. Every time he met with the Secret Service, and there had been a few occasions, Macleod wondered about the decision he made to recommend Kirsten Stewart for them. He always thought she could better them, make them a little less dispassionate, able to see other, better pictures. Looking at the scene in front of him, he wasn't so sure.

'Come on, McGrath, it's back to the bog-standard murders for us.'

Chapter 02

Kirsten pressed the red button on the remote control, switching off the television, and laid back in the arms of her man. She felt them snake around her, and she allowed him to roll his chin into the side of her neck, pulling her close. It had been three months since the shooting and she had received goodbyes from Dom and Kerry-Anne, who had disappeared off together, somewhere around the Caribbean, the last she'd heard. Not that she wished them any ill. In the short time that she had known them, they had come together to save her life on more than one occasion, but that was the past.

Craig tousled her hair and asked if she wanted another beer, but Kirsten shook her head. The trouble with alcohol in the afternoon was that you began to feel a little sleepy.

'I'll make a cup of coffee though,' said Kirsten, looking to roll away from him, but a pair of arms grabbed her back again. The couple kissed for several minutes before he allowed her to get up and walk over to the kitchen. Three months off work, despite the pain that had come from the shooting, meant that she'd been able to relax. Craig, of course, hadn't been there the whole time, but in the time that he had been, they'd made up for any time apart. As she stood making the coffee, she watched as he switched the television back on in that way that only men can do. He'd gone from being totally engaged in her to suddenly finding himself needing something to entertain him. She laughed a little as she ground up the coffee before tipping it into the empty filter paper. As she filled up the coffee machine with water, she heard Craig swear, something he was not particularly accustomed to.

'What's up?' asked Kirsten.

'This. That's the shopping centre in the middle of town,' said Craig. 'Isn't it? That's your one.'

Kirsten strode out from behind the kitchen area, round to the back of the sofa, peering at the television. Craig was right. It was the shopping centre in town. Kirsten could see the clock that entertained so many of the kids. The camera panned across showing the bullet holes that were in it, and a voice apologised and warned viewers in advance for some of the rest of the scenes that were there. Forensics were all over the scene, and Kirsten thought she caught a view of Jona Nakamura, the forensic lead at the Inverness police station.

She stared at the screen, searching to see if Macleod was there, her former boss, or maybe Hope McGrath, the red-haired six-foot sergeant, who had taken her under her wing when she first became a detective. She couldn't see either, although she didn't find that surprising, for Macleod was good at avoiding the cameras. He hated being in front of them. Detested them with a passion.

After a few moments, a picture of the Chief Constable came on telling everyone what a grievous incident it was. Giving some brief facts such as the time of the incident and the fact that a number of people were dead. Beyond that he said nothing, confirming no numbers.

Kirsten checked her phone, staring at it.

'What are you doing?' said Craig. 'You're not on duty. This is not yours to deal with. Just let it go.'

'I know, but I thought with Dom and Kerry-Anne out of the way, and a skeletal staff up at this end, that I might get a call. You're never really off duty in this job, are you?'

'Yes, you are. You're not signed on fit for duty. Therefore, you're not doing anything,' said Craig. 'Now, go back and make that coffee.'

'Don't,' said Kirsten. 'I want to see this.'

Craig raised his hands in defeat before leaning back on the sofa, letting Kirsten stare at the screen. There was another two minutes of reporting where a woman who had been in the shopping centre told of men firing guns, people hitting the floor, and blood running here and there. She said there'd been men, women, and children all around and she didn't know quite what had happened, for the shooting seemed to be coming from several different figures.

Kirsten took all this with a pinch of salt, for the report that had not been properly interrogated, and the press always picked out the best bits to sensationalise. *Trouble was*, she thought, *it was rather dour by comparison.* You really wanted a hysterical figure for your news report, not someone who seemed to be fairly calm. *Maybe it was because she got out alive*, thought Kirsten, *that she could be that calm. Maybe she hadn't seen any friends or family die.*

The news moved onto a report about a nuclear reactor and the upgrade it was receiving. Kirsten turned back and walked to the coffee machine. She realised she hadn't switched it on, for Craig had sworn before she'd done that. She now hit the button and stood waiting for it to complete. Craig looked over at her.

'Stop. It's not your problem. This is not one for you to do.'

'It's my town though. I could phone Macleod. I mean, I'm sure he'd tell me.'

'No,' said Craig. 'You took a bad one last time. Sure, you're up, you're on the move, but you're still not as frisky as you were before.'

'I thought I was frisky enough for you last night,' smiled Kirsten, giving a laugh and turning back to the coffee machine.

'But you're still not right,' said Craig. 'I know you're not, and they haven't signed you off, so at this point in time, you and I are taking time out. I'm on my leave, you are on special leave, so let's just leave it, shall we?'

Kirsten nodded, for he was right. She reached over to a hairbrush sitting in the kitchen and began brushing her hair back. It was true that she was getting back somewhere towards peak fitness, but she didn't feel she was sharp enough yet. She'd not only been exercising with Craig in the bedroom, he'd also been taking her out for runs, and down the gym. He'd even picked up a pair of sparring gloves for her. Unfortunately, he was no match and she really needed somebody to test her strength against. She thought about going back down to the mixed martial arts gym, but given the condition she was in, she wasn't sure Anna Hunt would have taken that too kindly. Kirsten lifted up her top, looked at the mark the bullet had left behind. The skin would never be the same. Neither would she. Maybe bikinis were out.

She heard footsteps behind her, and a hand went round and ran itself around her wound before lifting and embracing her in a completely different fashion. She laid back into him again, taking his advice, enjoying the time alone. She'd have taken her arm off for this quiet time previously and yet, there was part of her wanted back in the game. Still, it wasn't a bad way to spend your down time.

Kirsten realised that things were about to take a twist for the exciting when there came a knock at the door. Craig broke off his embrace, stepped back and she believed he swore again. Kirsten reached for the hairbrush, gave her hair a couple of strokes, put it down and walked over to the door. She glanced through the peephole and nearly swore when she saw who was standing outside. Craig wasn't going to be happy.

The door opened and Anna Hunt stepped into the room, looking immaculate in boots, a black skirt and a business-like jacket over the top.

'I thought you might call.'

'She's off duty,' shouted Craig. 'She's not ready. She needs more downtime.'

Kirsten wanted to turn around and tell Craig to keep out, mind his own business because she was desperate to get involved, but she knew he was protecting her and sometimes she needed protection from her own keenness.

'I'm afraid I need to talk to Kirsten alone,' said Anna. 'Business.'

'She's not signed back on,' said Craig.

'No, she's not,' said Anna, 'but I need to speak to her. If you don't mind.'

'Is the bedroom far enough,' said Craig. 'Should I hide in there?'

'The way you can hear and your skills, no it's not. Why don't you go get a coffee somewhere?'

'Why don't you get the hell out?' said Craig, causing Anna

to raise an eyebrow.

'I'll let that one slip, but just that one. You're still in my employ, no matter how much you care for this woman. Go get a coffee.' Craig looked over at Kirsten, who turned and walked towards him. She wrapped herself around him and whispered in his ear that it was okay. She'd tell him everything later on.

'Liar,' he said in her ear, 'you know you can't. Just be careful and don't do anything until you're ready.' With that he let the embrace slip, walked to the bedroom before emerging back out with his jacket around his shoulders. 'How long do you need?' he asked Anna Hunt.

'Just give us half an hour,' said Anna. 'For what it's worth, sorry.'

'I don't believe that for a minute,' said Craig. 'Just be gentle with her.'

Kirsten saw Craig walk to the door and slam it, making the point as he then disappeared down the stairs.

'You've really gone under his skin,' said Anna.

'And he, under mine,' said Kirsten. 'And he is right. I'm not signed back on duty. Why are you talking to me?'

'There's been an incident,' said Anna.

'Hell of an incident,' said Kirsten. 'I saw it. I think I saw Jona Nakamura on the TV; couldn't see Macleod.'

'I'm afraid Inspector Macleod has been removed from this one. Not his to follow up.'

'You've taken it?' queried Kirsten.

'Yes, we've taken it. You see the police think it's a crazy gun attack, but it's not. Looks like there's been a shootout, but I can't tell you here why.'

'You can't tell me here? You've just sent Craig off to have a coffee and yet you can't tell me what's going on?'

15

'No, not secure. I need you to retreat to a safe house. When you're there, we'll send a package with a detail and also your assignment.'

'My assignment?' said Kirsten. 'What, you going to have me chasing some people down?' Anna Hunt's face didn't flinch. 'Come on, Anna. I'm not ready yet. I'm not up to peak fitness.'

'People like you don't need to be at peak fitness. People like you are tenacious. That's why we brought you in. I can't wait on this one. I need somebody that knows the terrain up here. I need somebody who's able to act on their own and I need someone who I can trust.'

'Why trust? Surely, there's plenty of people you trust.'

'I trust your boyfriend,' said Anna, 'but he hasn't got the capacities I need.'

'I'm sure he'd be charmed to know, but why trust? We've got agents everywhere, plenty you could use. What's this about?'

'You won't know until the package arrives,' said Anna. 'Sorry, where are you going to go?'

'Where's the field of operation?'

'Currently, that shopping centre. We don't know a lot. We haven't got a lot to give you, but a lot will be in the package. You'll have to be operating out of Inverness.'

'Then I'll go to safe house seven on the edge. You know the address, don't you?'

'Yes, I do,' said Anna. 'That would seem a reasonable one to go to, but one thing you need to know, you cannot discuss this with Craig. You cannot discuss this with anyone.'

'I've got nothing to discuss at the moment,' said Kirsten.

'No, except that you're going to a safe house. Craig needs to know you're coming back. You can't hide that from him, but that's it. Nothing else.'

16

'I thought you said you trusted him,' said Kristen.

'Trust is a sliding scale. The moment you're involved, somebody knows that's your boyfriend. Somebody knows who to go after. When you're in bed together, you'll talk, you'll drop the odd thing. It happens to us all. You can try and focus on the physical, but we all need that connection, be it spiritual or be it emotional. We talk, we're human; therefore, Craig becomes a liability.'

'I would say much more than that.'

'But you're not a head of a department at the moment. You're on leave and that's why you're not thinking with your head.'

'He wouldn't cough anything up.'

'He would cough stuff up,' said Anna. 'I would. The techniques some of these people have, you can't stop it. All you can do is control the information and who's got it. Therefore, you can tell him nothing. This one's up at the top level. We're talking possible diplomatic problems with what's coming. I want you out of here in the next hour. I'll have the package sent over in two.'

'You don't really give me time to say long goodbyes, do you?'

'No,' said Anna. 'This is what we do.'

'Why aren't you doing it? I saw you last time. You can go with the best of them.'

'There's too many people know me on this one. I'd be marked. Besides, I've got plenty of other things I need to be doing.'

'It can't be that important, then, can it?'

'Let's just say my face doesn't fit this particular task,' said Anna. 'I've got a lot of history with a lot of people. As far as they're aware, you're the girl that comes running to the rescue. They got your picture when you stopped that train. When you

17

stopped the cruise ship, there were photographs. People are identifying you, but there you go. You're the hero. The person that steps in to prevent things. This time, however—' Anna Hunt's voice trailed off.

'Other work?' asked Kirsten.

'Our package will be with you, too. Stay safe. You report nothing to anyone except me, understood?'

'Of course,' said Kirsten, and Anna turned on her heel and walked to the door. She opened it, stepped out into the hallway and looked down to the stairs. 'Craig, you can come back up,' she said and heard the footsteps coming back.

Anna Hunt watched him walk past and into the flat, the man giving a cold stare at her.

'I'll leave you two together.' With that, Anna descended the stairs. Kirsten moved to close the door.

'That seems serious,' said Craig.

'I've got to be somewhere in an hour,' said Kirsten. 'Sorry, but you'll have to—'

'How long for?' asked Craig.

'Don't know. Haven't got instructions yet.'

Craig's eyes narrowed. 'She couldn't tell you the instructions here?'

'No.'

'And she couldn't handle it herself?'

'No, Craig. She just said she couldn't. It's on me.'

'She'll have told you not to talk to me,' he said. 'You're going to be out on a limb on this one. If you need me, you call, understand me? You call.'

Kirsten stepped forward, put her arms around her man and pulled him tight. 'I know,' she said. 'I know.'

Chapter 03

Craig told Kirsten that he would remain at her flat for the next five days because that's all the leave he had. After that, he would have to return to London. She thanked him, put her arms around him, kissing him once again. Having left the family of Macleod and McGrath and the rest of the police at the Inverness station, finding Craig had been a godsend. She felt she had some sort of stability in her life. Her previous rock or at least her previous devotion had been to her brother.

These days, she didn't visit him much because he didn't know her, his mind having gone. When he stood there questioning her, sometimes becoming enraged that she was in his room, Kirsten found it too hard to deal with. It was like somebody had died, and yet the person was still there. As much as she dealt with the horror of her new job and the terrible things that had gone on with it, she struggled to deal with the basic premise of dementia.

Kirsten had taken her car, parked it up away from her flat, and picked up a hire car, renting it for the next two weeks. It was from a company that was not particularly reputable, and she signed very little paperwork when she took it. Having checked over three cars at the site, she knew she had one that would respond if she put the foot down.

She parked on the edge of Inverness in what was a rather rough estate. Kirsten then walked to and entered a building that had the smell of blocked drains outside it. She'd chosen this building specifically because it looked a mess and had been cheap, but it wasn't the only safe house she knew of. She also had a few of her own. If her boss, Anna, wanted to send her a package, there was no way she was giving those up.

On entering, she went straight to the cupboard to find the coffee—instant—and boil the kettle before making her way to the patchy sofa and putting her feet up. There was nothing to do until the package arrived. She flicked on the battered old telly and sat, watching some soap, trying not to cloud her mind with news reports at this time.

She heard a knock at the door, jumped up from the sofa, and walked steadily over to look at the peephole. There was no one there. She drew a gun from behind her, opened the door slowly, and looked down to see a package resting on the doorstep. There were no postal marks on it, no address, nothing to indicate who it was for. Kirsten bent down, picked it up, and closed the door behind her, locking it tight. She placed the package on a little coffee table in front of the sofa and took out a small pen knife, cutting through the parcel's wrapping. She soon had the rather small box open to find a number of packages inside, one of which she recognised.

Looking at the size of the box, it looked like something that might contain about three or four decks of cards. This was ammunition; it was probably untraceable, certainly coming from a wide source. This did not bode well.

Kirsten took out the next package, opening it to find a mobile phone inside. This would be the contact for Anna. This one and nothing else. Kirsten's heart began to skip a beat. This really didn't look good. She reached inside and pulled out an A4 round tube. Taking the end off, she pulled out several pieces of paper and placed them in front of her. Holding them up, she read them briefly.

The subject matter of the paper was one Johann Stein. He was described as an Austrian scientist who was believed to have defected to Russia. There was a brief history of Stein. Highly thought of not only in the field of nuclear power, but also in weapons technology. He had worked for the services and had access to details about the UK's nuclear arsenal and their deployment abilities. It was these factors that meant any defection from him would be seen in a rather pale light. He'd seemingly disappeared several weeks ago, and all reports said he had gone to Scotland. It was believed that the shooting in the Inverness shopping centre had something to do with this, although details were still extremely sketchy.

Kirsten read on. It was advised that she should look out for Russian agents. At the moment, there was a manhunt going on from within the British forces. Anna Hunt felt that this would be unsuccessful and that they would need to find someone to delve deeper into the underground, reaching the Russians. At this time, there was one name that stuck out, an Orla Houghton, who may know of the man's trail and who he was using to evade the UK authorities. There had been a brief contact with her.

The source hadn't been seen by the service, but it was overheard by a third party on a phone line. It wasn't much to go on. Any other knowledge of his whereabouts was severely limited. The man had no friends or family in the north of

Scotland, but for some reason, he seemed to be operating there, and the gunfight in the Inverness shopping centre had confirmed it. Kirsten began to understand why Anna wanted to move quickly, but she didn't understand why Anna didn't trace the man herself. Three months previously, Anna had taken things in hand to deal with a dangerous rogue Russian agent.

Kirsten turned the page over, reading on into small details about the Austrian scientist's life before he worked for the service in the UK. Everything seemed to be based in Europe. Yes, you could run contact details, see if any of these people now operated within Europe, but Austria wasn't going to be harbouring them either. If this man was a traitor, surely these friends would be despising him. Kirsten read through their names, looked at them, and was struggling to see one as a defector.

There was a second sheet of paper. This was detailing the orders, not simply the information. Kirsten unrolled it and placed it in front of her. It simply said, *Target, Johann Stein*. The mission was to recover the scientist, but Kirsten looked beyond it. She saw a detail in red that she'd never seen in any of her previous orders. It advised that if the man wouldn't come in, he was to be eliminated.

Kirsten flopped back in her sofa.

Eliminated? Kirsten didn't do that. Kirsten was no assassin. Sure, she killed people. She had to; it was one on one. There were times when she was protecting other people, but this was an assassination. There were people within the service for this. People who could find, track down, and kill. Even if they couldn't find them, Kirsten could call them. Kirsten could say where the target was. Anna wanted her to approach him though; that was clear from the mission orders. She would try to reach out and bring him in. That would be preferable.

Kirsten left the instructions on the table, stood up, and walked over to the window. The curtains were drawn, and she pulled one back slightly, looking at the street below. There was no one moving, no one about. She turned, walked over to the kitchen, and opening one drawer, she took out a lighter. She walked back to the table and reached over for an ashtray, placing it in the centre. Kirsten didn't smoke, neither did anyone Kirsten knew on a personal basis, and since she'd worked from the safe house, there had never been smoke in it, yet there was always the ashtray. She took the detail in front of her, read it through again, memorising it before she ripped up the paper into small shreds. She then took the lighter, and after placing the paper in the ashtray, she set fire to it, watching it all burn.

'A kill order,' she said. 'A kill order.' Her hand reached down to her phone. Craig had said, 'Call.' Craig had said if she needed him. This should have been a simple instruction; these were her orders, but Kirsten didn't kill. Anna knew this, Kirsten was not one to kill. Why was Kirsten getting this? Why this assignment? When they first interviewed her, they asked her if she could kill, but she'd said quite plainly, she didn't know. If someone was facing her, if it were them or her, or someone else in the public domain, she believed she could pull the trigger.

If someone was defenceless, she'd apprehend; that was the police training. You apprehended the person. Yes, you might take more extreme measures if they were threatening someone else or someone else's life was in jeopardy, but you didn't just take them out. Besides, while she was in the police force, Kirsten didn't handle a weapon; she'd learned that when she'd joined the service.

She wanted Craig, or she wanted Macleod, someone to talk this through with. She couldn't phone Anna Hunt to talk about it. The meeting in her own flat had been evidence to that; she'd seen that Anna was agitated or at least nervous about giving this assignment out. Kirsten wandered back over to the sofa, threw herself down on it, and started looking at the ceiling. There were strips of wallpaper falling off it and a large patch of dump in the far corner. *Why me?* she thought. *Why me?*

She was also out on her own. She'd been told by Anna not to speak to anyone. It was implied that any rooting around on the internet would have to be done through a secure system, not one from the service.

Kirsten brought a name to mind, Martin Dunley. She knew it, though only vaguely. Dunley was somebody who relocated people. Someone who seemed to be something that she wasn't. Kirsten jumped up suddenly, deciding that being on the move was better. She needed to know more, understand what was going on before she simply refused an order. Anyway, it wasn't like that, was it? It wasn't a straightforward kill order; she'd have the opportunity to speak to the man, try to bring him in. She shook her head, letting her hair cascade down behind her.

She walked over to the cupboard and looked inside to see a range of clothing. It all fitted her, as she'd put it there two months previously. Slowly, she picked out what she wanted. There was a pair of leggings along with some baseball boots. She knew the look she wanted; it went along with the beat-up car that she had. She took a leather jacket throwing it over to the sofa before stripping down, putting on the clothing she'd brought out. She wore a simple black t-shirt and adjusted her holster so the gun couldn't be seen inside the jacket.

Happy that she was dressed to take on the world, Kirsten left the flat, walked down to the car, and turned on the engine. *Martin Dunley*, she thought and began to drive into the centre of Inverness. She stopped outside of a bookmaker's, Dunley's, and on entering, she looked up at the horse racing that was happening on the screens. Some old men looked over at her, wondering what she was doing here, but she almost grunted at them, forcing them to turn their attention back to their betting slips. She took one and wrote on it, *Anita wants to see you*, before marching up to the teller and placing it down in front of him. He took a look at it, gave a simple nod, and disappeared into the back room.

After a moment, the man waved her through, buzzing the security door to the side, allowing Kirsten to gain access. She walked through to the rear of the betting shop, through a wooden door, where a man with a few teeth missing smiled at her before closing it behind her. She sat down in a seat before a large wooden desk and a bald man on the far side. As she took her seat, he reached down to one of the drawers of the desk and held a gun up at her.

'Why is it we have a gunman rampaging, Anita, and you're here?'

Anita was an image that Kirsten had developed amongst certain parts of the underworld of Inverness. She was a rogue, someone who could play both ends, talk, and give information. Maybe it was a bit extreme what she was doing at the moment, but Kirsten needed information, and the man before her knew a lot more than anyone else.

'I'm not involved in the gunfight,' said Kirsten. 'It's not me. I've been asked by certain people to find out who it is. Find someone who might know. I need the whereabouts of that someone from you.'

'Why would you come here? Why would I know them? I don't keep with that sort of nonsense. I live here in Inverness; the last thing I want is a bloodbath.'

The man she was talking to was simply known as Jake, Jake the bookie. His real name was Martin Dunley, and he'd grown up within the Inverness underworld. He'd done well because he knew everything that was going on.

'Orla Houghton—where is she?' asked Kirsten. She felt a man put a gun in her back.

'Up, Anita. I need to make sure you're not carrying.'

Kirsten stood up, turned, and pushed the chair away, before raising her hands. The man with the gun at her back reached down into her jacket, at which point Kirsten turned, spun her hands around behind him, and twisting, threw him across her hip towards the other man in the room who was protecting Martin. The two of them cluttered together but Kirsten let powder go from inside her hand, a white powder that went straight to the eyes of Jake the bookie. By the time he'd recovered his sight, his two bodyguards were lying on the floor, and he had a gun being held over his head.

'Orla Houghton,' said Kirsten. 'And don't ever put a heavy on me like that again.'

Jake held up his hands, his own gun still in one, but his eyes were streaming.

'Okay,' he said. 'Okay. We're just a bit nervous with what's going on.'

'Orla Houghton, where? You'll have checked.'

'I have. Caledonian Canal on a boat.'

'Thank you,' said Kirsten. She reached over, took the man's gun, put it on the floor, and kicked it to the other side of the room before turning on her heel. She walked to the door, opened it, nodded to the teller crouching behind it after hearing the commotion. He walked her to the front door, holding it for her. A minute later, she was sitting in the car. *Caledonian Canal*, she thought. *At least we're on the move.*

Chapter 04

Kirsten drove her car down the side of Loch Ness where she stepped out along wooded areas, searching the loch with her binoculars. There was a photograph of Orla Houghton inside the package that had been delivered to the house. Kirsten remembered the face. She looked strange for what she did, someone who fixed it for criminals and other people to move about. False passports.

The woman had blonde hair, but not the straight kind. Vibrant, almost alive on her head. In the photograph, while shapely, she also had the clear look of someone who was a mother, and it was noted on the brief that she had seven kids. There was a man in the photograph with her, maybe her husband. Another man who looked out of shape and developing that middle-aged podge. There was certainly no high-class look about them, but then again, wasn't that the point? They just looked like anyone.

Nothing had ever been proven against the woman, but it was known that she operated in these fields. One of the things mentioned about Orla Houghton was the fact that she was happy to walk around in plain sight, probably giving her the best cover there was. A dedicated mother working alongside a man who drove a fork lift truck in a clothing factory. Hardly the stuff of legend, and certainly a good cover for a spy. The other thing about Orla was she wasn't connected specifically to the Russians, so Kirsten was having trouble working out why she would be involved in this instance. Wouldn't the Russians come in themselves and simply pick up Johann Stein if he was defecting?

It took Kirsten half a day to track down the boat, and it was only when she saw Orla's husband fishing off the back of it that she positively identified it. She watched it closely until it moored at the bottom of the Ford Augustus locks. From her vantage point, hidden in some bushes, she could see them serving the kids dinner and was really struggling to work out if she had the right couple. Yet the pictures matched.

Kirsten decided she would move in that night. The last thing she needed was a gunfight with kids caught in the crossfire, whoever they may belong to. At approximately one o'clock, Kirsten, still wearing her dark garb, calmly strode along the pontoons that the boat was tied up to. There were three other boats there, and she had to take care as one of them still had a man sitting on the outside. She waited until he turned his back, taking a sip from some wine. She scampered past.

The ability to move quickly but quietly was something they commented on when Kirsten was in training, but out in the field it all seemed so much more complicated. The pontoon moved as she raced along it and then more so as she leapt and swung herself up onto the back of the boat. It was a mid-size cruiser, and the rear doors led straight into the upstairs lounge, where she could see two kids lying asleep.

Quietly, she opened the door, stepped inside and took out her gun, almost feeling bad for Orla as she saw the kids sleeping. Slowly, she crept down the steps that led past a small galley and the table where the family would have eaten, until she reached the door at the fore of the vessel, which must have led through to the other sleeping quarters. Kirsten pulled the door back slowly, looking inside in the dark, but could see very little. She'd have to move quickly. She took a torch out and placed it in her hand, holding it along with the gun, ready to switch on the beam. She stepped inside the room, turned on the light, and saw two heads at the end of the bed. She jumped up onto the covers, and Kirsten placed her gun in the face of Orla Houghton who opened her eyes and went to scream.

'Don't,' said Kirsten. She swung one knee over, putting it into the solar plexus of Orla's husband. 'And you shut it. Don't say a word. Don't move or I fire this gun.'

'What are you doing?' said Orla in a frantic but hushed voice. 'My kids, why are you here?'

'Shut it,' said Kirsten. 'I don't want to hear that. I know who you are, Orla Houghton, and I know what you do. You're going to talk to me about Johann Stein.'

The woman continued to protest in hushed tones, saying to think of the children behind her. Kirsten put the gun closer to the woman's face. 'Start talking.'

Kirsten saw Orla's husband begin to reach round with his hand towards her, and she quickly took her hand off her torch, swinging across and catching the man on the jaw, the gun continuing to be held in the face of Orla.

'Don't,' said Kirsten. 'I don't want to kill you, but I will do if necessary.'

Kirsten wasn't too sure if she could live up to this statement, considering the fact that they were unarmed but she made sure that the doubts were not shown on her face. Instead, she adjusted her knee on the husband's body, pushing down into his chest, causing him to start to wheeze.

'Okay, just ease up on him.'

'Start talking and I'll ease.'

'Okay. Johann Stein comes to me four weeks ago; says he needs passports out of the country. Not a problem. Do that for a lot of people.'

'Why is he coming to you?'

'Because he knows I'm the best. I'll get him past anywhere.'

'But the Russians are after him; the Russians want him. Did they talk to you? Did they pay you money?'

'No,' said Orla. 'It was him directly. Stein came directly to me, paid me cash.'

'And he never mentioned Russia?' asked Kirsten.

'No,' said Orla. 'Look, I'll tell you, for God's sake. Just take it easy. I've got kids up there.'

'I know,' said Kirsten. 'Maybe you should be in a different line of work but keep talking. Where did he want to go?'

'No idea. I did him a Hungarian passport though.'

'Okay, so what, he's on the move to Hungary?'

'I don't know,' said Orla Houghton. 'Look, take it easy. Can we get up, go through, and talk quietly in there? This is not a good position.'

'No, but it's my position and I'm on top,' said Kirsten. 'So, no, we can't move. You're not my friend. I want information from you. If you're lucky I'll leave you alone, but unless you tell me what I want to know . . .'

'Okay,' said Orla, her hand starting to come up from underneath the bed clothes. 'Okay, just relax.' Kirsten held the light at Orla's face, but her eyes kept darting towards the husband. He was in a much fainter light at the side of where the torch was being shone.

'So, what happened at the shooting?'

'I don't know. Nothing to do with me,' said Orla, 'but I tell you this, I'm not going near him. I thought it might have something to do with him.'

'Why?' asked Kirsten.

'You're not the first person to pay a visit, but they were much more subtle. Bus stop in Inverness. Somebody came up and asked me, gun in my back, kid sitting beside me. He's too hot. I don't want anything else to do with him. Still owes me money, but I don't want it. I said I don't want anything.'

'The person that spoke to you. Foreign?'

'Yes.'

'Russian?'

'Couldn't say. Eastern bloc accent behind it. Tried to sound very English, which I don't know why they did that. We're in Scotland here.'

'What did they ask you, specifically?' asked Kirsten.

'Similar to you. Where's he going? What passports did he get?'

'It doesn't make sense though,' said Kirsten. 'I mean, if he's with the Russians, he'd have gone by now. You can get through from Hungary.'

Orla Houghton laughed. It wasn't a simple laugh, but quite loud. Kirsten pushed the gun forward.

'Quieter,' she said. 'You keep it quiet. Don't try that one.'

'Okay,' said Orla. 'Okay. I'm laughing because you all think he's off to Russia, but he paid me on his own. Didn't see any Russians involved. I've worked for them before. I'm not, to be candid, proud of my country. I'll happily take whoever pays me. The Russians have paid me a couple of times, but I'm sure you guys know that. Probably why you're speaking to me at the moment. Who said where I was? Jake was keeping tabs on me. Did you do this to Jake?' Orla smiled. 'I hope you busted his face. He's been a pain in the arse, that man, to me.'

Kirsten was unsure what was going on, but she also wasn't sure she was getting told the truth. 'So, what's happening?' asked Kirsten and she swapped the gun over in her hands, pointing the torch now into the face of Orla and putting her gun between the legs of the woman's husband. 'Seriously, what's going on?'

'Okay,' said Orla. 'Don't do that to him. You have no idea how that makes men feel.'

'I think I do. Why do you think I'm doing it?' asked Kirsten. 'Tell me. Stop talking about me and him and what I'm doing and tell me what Johann's doing.'

'Well, Stein comes to me. He asks for the passports to Hungary. That's all legit. Gave me the money.'

'Did he ask specifically for Hungary? I don't think so. I think you've sent him there.'

'I told him to go to Hungary because ultimately he's looking to get to South America, possibly further.'

'Where's further than South America?' asked Kirsten.

'Colonies down in the Antarctic. He's going to hide away on an expedition down there or something. That's what he was talking about. Find some berth on a ship or something. Keep right out of the limelight for a couple of years. He was worried, though, I can tell you that. He was worried. Normally people like this, I just jump in and charge them double what I normally would because they want to haggle. Those in the business, they know my rates, they just do it. They know how good I am. People like this, they don't. They're trying to haggle

33

down, but he just agreed. Not a problem.'

'How much?' asked Kirsten.

'Fifty K. Wasn't even a rush job.'

'Okay,' said Kirsten, 'and how good was it? How accurate were your documents?'

'Perfect,' she said. 'I mean, he should be gone by now. He would have been gone long before Inverness and the shooting.'

'That's why you're bothered,' said Kirsten. 'That's what worries you. He's sticking around and he's attracting a lot of heat and you could get caught up in that.'

'I am getting caught up in it,' said the woman. Kirsten stared into her eyes and was once again amazed by how homely she looked. This did not look like any sort of master criminal, but rather someone that barely knew about the underworld at all. Yet, according to the records, she was one of the best operators going.

'Okay. Say I believe you. What's he up to? Why has he not left?'

'You search me. He didn't strike me as a collaborator. He didn't strike me as someone trying to get to Russia, and yes, you're right. If they were getting him out, they've got their own people. They can afford to do things better than me. Well, at least that's what they think, but they've never matched me in this capacity. It's usually for people who are coming in from their services, trying to get in, get out, not for somebody who's being extradited, being pulled out. Meet him on the coast, get away on a boat or something. Why bother flying straight over to Russia, taking the risk, going through authorities, the tickets? No, he would've been known.'

Kirsten thought, *Well, Anna Hunt knew that all that was going on. The authorities would've known. They'd have been looking for him in CCTV, through the airports, through the ports. Orla was right; his best bet would've been to go to the coast and take a boat or take a plane from somewhere small.*

Slowly Kirsten started to inch her way back off the bed. 'Wrap yourselves up,' she said. 'Nice and tight to each other. I want to see the hands behind each other's heads.' Kirsten watched the couple perform the most nervous hug of their life. As she got to the door, she advised them to remain in that position for the next five minutes.

'I'll be walking past your kids. Don't try anything. I've no malice towards them. Be a shame.'

Kirsten crept backwards up the steps to the rear of the vessel, then out and onto the fore deck. The neighbour had gone inside, the light still showing inside his vessel, but clearly the night air was not being appreciated with his wine. By the time that Kirsten reached her car and fired it up to drive back to the safe house, she had more questions in her head than any answers.

Stein had clearly some agenda here, and someone had an agenda for Stein. There was a bloodbath in a shopping centre. It was very un-agency, whether it be her side or another. The man had the passport. He should be gone, especially if he was going to go through the airports. Why hang about? Was something keeping him here? If it was Russia, he could get a boat or a plane. He could get a sub to pick him up off the coast if he was that precious. They could make things happen. Nothing seemed to have happened except for people coming after him.

She drove through the dark roads along the side of Loch Ness, twisting here and there. Kirsten began to wonder. *On my own*, she thought. *Why on my own? If this is a man hunt, and if he's just got as much information as Anna talked about, why am I on my own? Why is it not a team effort and why not have a specialist with me? Someone who could pick him off from a distance?* She'd only begun investigating and already Kirsten had more questions than answers.

Chapter 05

Kirsten was in a quandary. She had followed up the lead of Orla Houghton and had come up with a dead end. Johann Stein had gone to ground. Despite spending the next day in front of a computer, she could find little trace of him. Sure, there were old records and she managed to break in and find out his security settings within the service, but they only told her so much. After all, there was only so far she could get through into the system without being flagged. Her instructions were to be covert, not to speak to anyone, and that implicitly meant not bringing any attention to herself.

After having a shower in the safe house, Kirsten sat on the grubby sofa thinking about her next move. What did she actually have? Some detail from Anna that the man was wanted, being chased by Russians, confirmation from Orla that he'd been given a passport, but it seemed that he hadn't left the country. There was a shootout supposedly involving him. Kirsten had confirmation of that, but it seemed to be the only part of the story she hadn't investigated fully.

Part of that assumption was that Anna would be all over it. She'd taken over the investigation from Macleod and the rest of the Inverness Police Force, and therefore any relevant detail from it would have been given to Kirsten. However, with what was going on, Kirsten was beginning to question that. There was also the fact that she was put on a kill order. If it came to that, Kirsten was going to need a lot more information about what was going on. She wasn't an assassin; she would need some sort of justification for her actions.

Kirsten wanted a source of information for the shootings, and realised she couldn't go back inside the service, as they would have eyes everywhere and be questioning why she was doing it; why she didn't simply believe when they were supposedly giving her full information.

Kirsten would also be breaking the rules. She was meant to be silent, and maybe that was also against her own service. Maybe there were ears there that shouldn't hear things. She'd run across this before. Kirsten realised from the television that the local police force had been there. Macleod had been involved, maybe Hope, Jona certainly. The trouble was that these were high-profile figures these days. Macleod struggled to go about town without someone recognising him, having been involved in so many high-profile cases. Hope was getting that way too, the tall redhead at Macleod's shoulder. If truth be told, he always seemed to bump her forward for interviews. The man hated dealing with the press as she knew only too well from her time working with him.

No, she couldn't go to them. She could go to the new sergeant she'd met, Clarissa Urquhart. She didn't know her that well, and certainly didn't believe she could put her full trust in her. If Urquhart kicked it upstairs, who knew how Anna Hunt would react. There was another member of the team, though, one that she did trust, one that she'd worked with closely at the station while on the murder squad. Alan Ross, the efficient, almost machine-like man behind the unit, the one that held it together, made sure the paperwork was done. Someone that Kirsten thought Macleod would struggle to work without.

It would have to be Alan, but she'd have to be careful. The last thing she needed was him being brought into any of this. She thought about where he went, his normal routine. He did have a partner at home, a male partner, but he also liked the clubs. Nothing too loud and ridiculous, but sometimes he just needed to get out into his own crowd.

Kirsten remembered his favourite haunt, near the centre of Inverness. Donning her usual black jacket, Kirsten walked down to the car, driving out towards the city centre before parking up in a backstreet. Ross lived in the centre of the city in a flat with his partner. Kirsten stood across the road from it watching it for nearly half an hour and tried not to look conspicuous. The flat had little cover around it and she was glad when she clocked Alan Ross coming down the stairs and on to the street.

He was spruced up in his jeans, a lilac shirt on top, and Kirsten walked at a discreet distance behind him, but in truth, she knew where he was going. She followed him through the city centre streets, taking a left and a right and then down through a small alleyway to the door of a club. From the outside, it looked like any other nightclub, but it wasn't, being much subtler like that, more like a pub. But it was a pub for a man of a particular appreciation.

Once Kirsten had seen Alan go inside, she walked past the man on the door and round to the rear of the building. Everywhere always had a back entrance, there was always somewhere where you could step inside without being seen, and this particular building was no exception. There were two large bins sitting outside, green and long, with sliding back lids, and they stank. Kirsten stepped around them and saw a back door that was lying ajar. She slipped inside, looked left and saw a kitchen area with food being prepared and headed immediately away from it, down a corridor and past a couple of offices. Beyond that, she saw a door leading to where a lot of noise was coming from.

It was good-natured, with music being played on a reasonably loud sound system. When she opened the door and peered in, she saw many men sitting in different booths, but she caught one on his own. The lilac shirt was there, and in front of him was a paper. *Probably doing a sudoku*, thought Kirsten, remembering fondly back to the days when Ross would be the one showing her how the systems worked. She'd come on some distance since then, but she'd never forgotten him. In truth, he'd been even kinder than Macleod and Hope had been, and the pair of them had worked together well as a team.

Kirsten opened the door, closed it gently behind her, and walked across the wooden floor of the club, sitting down in the booth opposite Alan Ross. He glanced up and then his face broke into a smile.

'What are you doing here?' he asked and watched as Kirsten scanned around her. Nobody seemed interested.

'I need your help. Sorry. It's been a long time and I should have popped by before, but right now, I need your help.'

Alan went to fold away his paper. Kirsten reached forward with her hand, stopping him, and told him to continue doing his sudoku. 'I don't want this to seem like it's a big thing. Just an old friend dropping in to say hello.'

'If it's that bad,' said Ross, 'why don't you go and see the boss?'

'I can't go to Macleod or Hope; they're too high-profile. I needed to speak to somebody on the quiet. Not many people come in here that don't need to. I kind of guessed you'd be able to spot them.'

'Well, you'd probably be spotted. Don't get that many women in here. We do get some. You are looking well though,' said Ross. Kirsten knew it was a genuine compliment. For all that Ross had an affection for her, it was simply that, the affection of a friend. In many other places, people would give compliments and, in their minds, probably had other ideas or thoughts running through them. Ross was never like that. Kirsten loved it about the man.

'Were you on scene the other day with the shootings?' asked Kirsten.

'Briefly,' said Ross, 'but that's been handed over to your lot, hasn't it? I mean you're going to know more than I do.'

'Pretend I don't,' said Kirsten. She put her hand forward, taking Ross's in it. 'Just talk like we're good old friends.'

'Well, we got there, and the place was a mess. The first units that arrived had a hell of a problem. From what I could gather from my early interviews, there was somebody running through the area, and gunshots were exchanged, but they were being fired between different parties. It wasn't just one. A lot of public talk about who were then dragged away. Security managed to get a lot of them into the shops and put the barriers down in front, which they reckon saved quite a few lives.'

'Think it was a crazy gunman?' asked Kirsten.

'No, no more like gang rivals.'

'What sort of gang?'

'Well, that was the thing,' said Ross, 'from the clothing as it was described, you wouldn't pick them out from anybody else that was in the shopping centre.'

Kirsten thought that would be her. That's what the services would be like, people you wouldn't know from Adam, just heavily armed and ready to kill. 'Tell me more.'

'Well, there's not that much to say. Most of the people on the scene were local, except for a couple. Some of the bodies that were there, at least two people, we didn't know at all. We never got time to fully identify them before your boss came along, closed off the scene. From one of the witness descriptions, though, one of the bodies was pulled away. Taken.'

'Taken? Where?' asked Kirsten.

'Just gone, gone off the scene, but definitely was there initially. Shot dead, bullet through the head and then removed from the scene.'

'That sounds like my unit or the side I work on. Gangs wouldn't do that. Not in the middle of a firefight.'

'That's what I thought, as did the boss, and there was no surprise when your people came in and took over. You're telling me you don't know anything about it? I thought you were well up in this part of the world.'

'I'm the north of Scotland section head, Alan,' said Kirsten, giving details she'd given to no one else, such was her trust in Ross. 'But I got shot several months ago, in an incident. Been off for a while, and I've been tasked back into something to do with this. I can't tell you anymore. In fact, I wasn't too happy about coming here.'

'Well, stay for a bit, make it look like a proper old friends' visit. I'll get us a couple of drinks.'

Ross stood up, made his way over to the bar while Kirsten

sat back in the booth, letting her eyes wander around the room, but not staring intently. Over by the bar, she saw someone dressed in a dark coat with a whisky in front of him. It was a little bit unusual and the club was warm, so that even she had thought about taking off her jacket, never mind a long coat. Kirsten had to cover up her weapon, however.

When Ross came back with the drinks, Kirsten began to talk to him about his current life. Mostly it was just to glean about the incident, but she wanted to stay for a while, follow Ross's lead, making it look like a proper old friends' reunion. After all, anybody checking her up would know that Ross had worked with her.

'Have you seen much of your brother these days?' asked Ross.

'No,' said Kirsten. Her brother was in an institution and didn't even know her. She often hadn't time to visit him, but she knew Macleod had done so.

'I was in last week,' said Ross. 'He's okay. Well, I say he's okay. Do you know what I mean? He doesn't know anybody and that, but well, he's healthy.'

'I find it hard to visit him,' said Kirsten. 'He's not like somebody I know, and he doesn't know me. All the little things when we used to see each other, all the things that made it look like we were close, they're gone.'

'You're truly on your own then?' Ross looked up at her and then smiled. 'You're not, are you? You're not. Who is he? Some dark, tall, handsome stranger, no doubt.'

He wasn't that tall, and his hair wasn't that dark but Kirsten had found him handsome.

'I can't tell you who he is, but he's good for me. He's very good for me.' They talked about nothing for the next half an hour, before Kirsten stood up and they embraced. As they hugged, Alan whispered in her ear, 'Stay safe, and if you need me . . .'

'I know,' said Kirsten and turned and walked over to the bar before leaving. She took up a position beside the man in the dark coat and almost pouted forward.

'I thought this was a bar for gay men,' she said to the man. He looked back at her.

'It is,' he said.

'Well, all you've done is stare at me. You must like what you see.' Kirsten reached forward with her hand, stroking his shoulder, before coming in behind him, and putting her other hand on his other shoulder. She pressed gently against the side, confirming the weapon that was hiding underneath his coat.

'I'm not looking for that sort of thing,' said the man roughly, shrugging her off.

'Easy then, no need to be like that.' Kirsten turned on her heel, walking out of the door.

She was bothered about the man. Once she'd exited, she loitered in an alley across the road. The man emerged only five minutes later, and he seemed in a desperate hurry. Kirsten pulled her jacket around her. They'd been tailing her. Somebody had been tailing her and now she wanted to find out who.

Chapter 06

Kirsten kept at a distance, tailing the man back into the city centre before watching him jump on a bus. At this point, she had to sprint, trying to time him sitting into a seat with her getting on to pay and then taking up a position where he couldn't see her. It was an artform she'd had to learn, but at least the worst that could happen was she'd be clocked enough to give up the chase. They were out in the open after all, but her mind thought back to the Inverness Shopping Centre.

That was in the open and that was full-on and bloody. Who exactly were they dealing with who would cause such devastation? Part of her now wondered if it had been wise to even go and see Alan, but she had nothing, nowhere to go, nothing to look at and yet still had a man to trace. Johann Stein, defector; it still didn't ring true for her.

The bus bumbled its way out through the city to the edge and cut into an estate that Kirsten recognised. It was due to be made over and delays had been made to the planning. Most of the residents had cleared out off to different kinds of housing, fresher, neater, more environmentally friendly. The few that remained were those that had refused to shift, usually too caught up in a drug-induced euphoria. She watched the man step off the bus out into this bleak landscape. The day was beginning to darken and Kirsten kept a wide berth of the man as he made his way along three different streets before turning into a house. It was a semi-detached, but had been converted to flats, one upstairs, one downstairs on either side. She saw him coming up to the front door of the lower flat, which was opened, allowing him access before he'd even knocked. Kirsten held her ground, watching from a distance with a small set of binoculars she kept inside her jacket.

It was another three hours before darkness had fallen completely and she saw lights on the side of the house. The upstairs, however, was dark, as were the two flats on the other side of the semi-detached building. Kirsten quietly walked along the street before cutting in three houses beforehand and rooting through the back gardens. Many were overgrown. One had a tricycle lying in the middle of it, which she nearly fell over.

As her eyes were now well-adjusted to the dark, she was able to get to the rear of the building in question. One thing Kirsten was aware of was that there may be somebody upstairs, a guard of some sort without any lights on or indication they were there. That's what she would've done, posted somebody up there or at least cameras. However, it was a risk she was willing to take for she had no idea how many people were downstairs.

Approaching the door of the upstairs flat, Kirsten took out some lockpicks and, within thirty seconds had opened the door. Having put her equipment away, she drew her gun and slowly stepped inside, closing the door behind her. She didn't turn on any lights, but her nose fought against the smell that spoke of damp and mildew. She believed the carpet below her was a dark blue and she crouched as she climbed stairs up into the flat above.

At the top of the stairs was another door. Slowly she opened it, keeping her back to the wall. Once inside, she didn't dare bring her torch out because that would be an obvious indication to her actual location. Instead she scouted, finding first the bedroom on the right-hand side. There was nothing there, just a mattress, the place obviously having been gutted. She entered a small lounge area, again, with nothing inside. At the rear was a bathroom. Again, it stank, and she could see where the mildew had climbed the walls. *How long has this been sitting empty?* she thought. Maybe downstairs had been derelict before as well and they had just occupied it.

Having scoured the upstairs flat, Kirsten set to work and listened initially through the floorboards to the ceiling below and to the noises that were coming through. She could hear a television and as she moved to other rooms, she heard conversations. Kirsten reached inside her jacket, taking out a small pen device that had a tiny drill on the end of it. She made for one of the corners of her room and turned on the drill device. It spun almost silently.

She lifted up the carpet and allowed the device to slowly penetrate, creating the smallest of holes. From inside her jacket, she took a long wire and attached one end to her phone. She dropped the other in through the hole so it had barely peeked out at the other side. With a few taps on her phone, she got an image for what was below. More than that, a small microphone that was at the end of the wire was able to pick up sound and Kirsten listened closely with an earpiece plugged into her phone.

The room contained three men and they began to talk in Russian. Kirsten's language skills were not great, but she could see they were having an argument about something. One of the men was the one she'd approached in the bar. As they sat talking with beers in front of them, she could see automatic weapons stored in the corner.

They weren't simple high-powered handguns, something you could discreetly conceal. Instead, some of these were large, high-powered rifles. After watching them for a period and getting no further, Kirsten moved to a different room and produced another hole through which to watch. This time, she'd found the kitchen, where a man was preparing food. It was unusual to eat this late at night, but Kirsten also kept a watch on the door from the upper window of the flat she was in. People were coming back and forward at an alarming rate. She reckoned there must be at least ten people in the house.

Around two in the morning, she moved to another room and found a lot of men sleeping. A fourth hole created half an hour later showed her a room with several computers. At that point in time, they were all blacked out, laptops closed. As people slept, Kirsten pondered her next move. Clearly, there was the chance that something could be discovered here, but they were almost exclusively talking in Russian, a language that she did not have a lot of knowledge of.

She was also aware that the bulk of them were asleep, so she crept over to her own bedroom and pulled at the mattress, only to find that it was damp in the middle. She dragged it through quietly into the main living room area, which seemed to be one of the drier parts of the flat. She turned the mattress over before walking to the bathroom and checked that the tap worked. She opened it slowly to see if the pipes would make a noise. Once she was happy they didn't, Kirsten stripped off and gave herself a cold wash.

She had to shake herself dry, and having done that, she dressed again, re-entered the main room where she now had laid the mattress and spread herself on top of it, a jacket over the top of her body. She would sleep the way she'd been taught to, like a sentry, always ready for the movement, always ready to hear. Tomorrow morning, she would look more closely, see if she could hear anything or discover anything more before deciding on her next move.

As Kirsten drifted off to sleep, she thought about Craig. He'd still be in her flat. That's what he said he was going to do, stay there for the rest of his trip until he had to go back down to London. Part of her ached to just creep back out of this flat, head over there for the night before returning in the early hours of the morning. She checked her watch.

It was the early hours of the morning and Anna had given her instructions not to see anyone, or rather not to talk to anyone about the mission. She knew if she saw Craig, he'd ask and eventually he'd get something out of her, and that could put him at risk. Instead, Kirsten cuddled herself, wrapping her knees up with her arms, tucking herself into a tight ball. She closed her eyes, but she was aware of what was going on around her, and then took six hours sleep, fading in and out.

When she finally woke up to full awareness, Kirsten stood up and shook herself out. There was movement downstairs, and she spent the first two hours going from room to room, counting the number of people who were occupying the building downstairs. She counted ten again. That was a large force. Clearly, Johann Stein was a big enough target to involve this many people, but it also spoke of a squad, that if they saw him, they could move and kidnap him.

It didn't sit well with Kirsten. If Stein was on the run and looking to defect, it would've been done with a handful of people that had kept it quiet, not brought in this sort of number. Depending on how they came in at the borders, somebody would have been aware that there was a presence in the country.

As it got towards midday, Kirsten began to get peckish, her stomach growling. She thought about leaving and getting some supplies and coming back, but the time to do that was night time, not now in the middle of the day. Besides she didn't want to miss any of the activity.

All the laptop screens were now open, but she was struggling to see them. Kristen sat watching the screens, heard numerous conversations in Russian, but not picking up any names that she needed. She was almost relaxed in what she was doing, but then her ears picked up when she heard something downstairs.

She'd moved the mattress back earlier on in the day, knowing that if anyone arrived, she wanted the flat to look exactly as when she'd entered it. She quickly covered up the hole with the carpet, tucked her phone inside her jacket, along with the wiring, and pulled out a weapon. She could hear Russian being spoken. There were two people coming up the stairs into the flat. Kirsten had decided where she would go and crept into the stinking bathroom, for up above the door was a shelf, presumably where they put towels and the unused toilet roll.

She had tested it and it seemed reasonably sturdy, so she'd hold herself up, lying on her side above the door. She heard laughter and then doors opening and closing before someone opened the bathroom door. Beneath her was a head of black hair, and she watched as the man stepped forward and pulled down his zip to begin to urinate in the toilet. Her heart skipped a beat, for if he turned, he would see her above the door. Kristen was unaware where the other man was, but she'd be ready for him if he saw her.

Knowing if the man who was at the toilet would turn that he would see her, Kirsten decided to take a risk. She grabbed the edge of the shelf she was leaning on, rolled and then spun her feet round to the ground, landing lightly, and then stepping quickly around the corner into the bedroom. On the far wall was a wardrobe that had almost collapsed, and Kirsten quickly hid inside it.

She heard some Russian, something to do with not being finished yet, and then a second man entered the room she was hiding in. She watched him go to the mattress, lift it up and then search around the room. As he came to the derelict wardrobe, she heard him choke and cough before he moved off in another direction. Kirsten stood up, continuing to listen, until she heard the door being closed at the front of the flat.

Slowly, she came out, clearing every room as if she expected an enemy to be in it. Only when she got to the front door and then checked the stairs did she begin to relax, putting her gun away, back inside its holster. Clearly, they were worried that people were looking for them, and she'd have to be on her guard.

Returning to her work, Kirsten rolled up the carpet, put down the small camera and audio microphone, and began listening to the Russian being spoken below. All the names she heard were Russian. Johann Stein was not mentioned. None of her own service were mentioned. Neither was Alan Ross and this she considered a good thing.

As she sat there listening, she found herself having to contain her hunger, but she knew by tonight, it will have been well over twenty-four hours since she'd eaten. In the early hours of the morning, she would sneak out and get something. Kirsten settled herself down.

She thought of Craig back at her flat. Surely there was a better life than this. Everything with Craig seemed to be part-time, and on the run, but she realised if they ever actually were to get together properly, and she meant actually living full time with each other, it would be outside the service. It was a thought she knew she shouldn't be entertaining while she was working. In truth, she had maybe another twelve or thirteen hours before she'd even think about going out for food. She had to dwell on something to keep the hunger away.

Chapter 07

It was two in the morning before Kirsten dared to venture out. Nearly everyone downstairs had gone to sleep with only one person up on guard duty. They had taken up a routine of stepping outside about once an hour, and Kirsten waited until they'd completed that before descending the steps out of the flat. She disappeared round the back of other semi-detached houses, before emerging out on the street some distance away. She was more than aware that it was early in the morning, and her best bet for food was an all-night garage, or possibly one of the superstores.

Rather than make for a taxi, Kirsten hiked just over four miles to come to an all-night superstore, where she stocked up with some sandwiches and some drinks, half of which she consumed before she'd left the car park. She then strode back to her car, which had been left in the town, and drove it to the location about half a mile away from the flat she had been watching. It was around five-thirty in the morning when Kirsten returned and snuck back up to the upstairs flat. She briefly checked what was happening downstairs, finding another person up keeping watch, before she went to the mattress and tried to get a disturbed sleep for a couple of hours.

By nine o'clock she was tired, but at least she was no longer hungry, and she had fluid on which to sip. Kirsten returned to her habit of going round to the different holes she created, putting the cameras down and discovering what everyone was up to downstairs. It was during one of these routines that she was looking in the rooms with the laptops and two words were heard as distinct as day, 'Johann Stein.'

The person who said it was indicating to a colleague at something on the screen. Her Russian, not being what it could be, Kirsten did overhear the term for tracker. The hairs on her neck picked up. Were they going for him? She needed to get down there to see where it was, because the camera angle she had was too far away on a tiny camera to pick up the detail of the screen. Kirsten thought about the room, where it was located, and how to get in. It would be awkward when you had three people working computer screens, but she was aware over the last couple of days that they stopped to have lunch together.

Sure enough, the man in the kitchen was preparing food and they would take it through to the front room, briefly leaving the computer desk unmanned. During this time, she could get in. If the downstairs had roughly the same geometry as upstairs, then she may have to come in through one of the windows. It was a risk, but Kirsten thought it was worth taking. She consumed the rest of her food while she waited for their lunch to be ready. Slowly, they all stood up, disappearing into the front room.

Using the camera, she could see the chef taking the food through. Quickly, Kirsten crept downstairs out from her own flat, routing to the outside of the building. It was now daylight.

She was a dark-haired woman, standing in a leather jacket, dark leggings underneath and surely would be asked by anyone what on earth she was doing there.

Kirsten crouched down, tight up against the wall, skirting round until she was underneath the window where the computer room should be. Slowly, she looked up, but there were curtains pulled across. Obviously, they wouldn't sit and let everyone see how many people were working in there.

She found the window to be an old sash type, so took a knife from her jacket. Placing the knife underneath the frame, she was able to lever it, pushing the window up. Clearly these buildings were so old, they needed changing. Maybe the sash window had been put in as a nod back to grander days, but in truth, the whole flat just looked ridiculous, a mishmash of ages. With the window jimmied up, Kirsten hurled herself up and through, landing on the carpet as quietly as she could, and then replacing the window to its original position.

The laptop screens were closed. She walked over to the one the man who had given the name Johann Stein had been sitting behind. She opened it up and saw a screensaver and gently tapped the mousepad on the front of the laptop. The screen changed, and she could see the dashboard of a tracking software. It was in Russian, so she had no idea what it said, but there was a red dot that was constantly moving.

She stared at the map in front of her, in black and white, and tried to locate where she was. She recognised the name of Carrbridge. It was somewhere south of Inverness. Then she saw an area, fenced off, but of such large space, it must be some sort of an estate. She checked the road that was running up one side, and the smaller roads coming off it. There was a park, a fun park, outside Inverness. She recognised it immediately.

What on earth was he doing there? Why was Johann Stein in there? She'd need to move quickly.

Kirsten closed the laptop down and went to move back for the window, but she heard movement. She glanced around the room, seeing a wardrobe behind her, old and wooden, clearly in disrepair, but it was the only cover in the room, other than going underneath the tables on which the laptops sat. She stole across, opened the wardrobe, closing it behind her, and crouching down so she could look out through the keyhole. She could hear the door open, and several footsteps entered the room, dull and heavily masked by the carpet. Then they began to chitchat in Russian. Johann Stein was mentioned several times. Kirsten could see the men walking to the far corner, picking up the large automatic weapons, checking them over.

But one thing was puzzling her. Why such heavy armoury? Once again, the thought occurred to her, *Were these people here to kill? To take out?* If you were going to extradite, you didn't come in this heavy handed. You came in quiet. These people seemed to be wanting the man at all costs. What was it that Stein knew? Anna Hunt had said that he was in the possession of secrets regarding the UK's nuclear arsenal and their deployment abilities. So clearly, he would be a good target, but not for this. Not for open bloodbath.

Also, if that was the case, why hadn't the government called it? Why hadn't they turned around and said this was Russians? There was no reason to cover it up. No reason to hide. Something was bothering Kirsten about this. Something wasn't right. Until she knew what, it was time to get on with the job. The current job was how to get out of this room with three people sitting in it.

Of course, there was no way to move out without opening

fire. As far as she knew, no one knew she was onto them. If Johann Stein escaped from the fun park he was in, Kirsten could come back again, see if these people knew how to track him. Clearly, something was up. They had placed the tracker on him somehow. Were the agents out working, looking to make an easy grab? Once again, her mind was confused. There was a mix here between stealth and firepower that didn't seem right. The men rather abruptly stood up, walked over to the guns they'd been working with previously, and started packing them into bags. Then they left the room all of a sudden. Kirsten listened to the commotion coming from the front room.

They were planning and maybe they'd be leaving soon. Kirsten stepped out of the wardrobe and walked through the end of the room listening to what was being said in the front room. It was all in Russian, but again, several times, Johann Stein was mentioned. Kirsten walked back over to the window, took out her knife, slid up the sash, and stepped out before moving it back down. As she finished putting the sash down, she heard the front door open from the downstairs flat and she quickly ran to the rear of the house. From there, she peeked and saw three men with large black bags move out to a car that had just pulled up.

Of course, they were sensible enough not to keep their car at the building, where it would've looked wholly out of place. It was a minivan. She didn't think it could hold everyone that was in the building at this time. Surely they all wouldn't leave, not until the job was done. Another two men stepped out, one of whom spoke to the other as she watched the instructed man moved off to the front of the building. The man who'd given instructions now came down the side of the building towards where Kirsten was lurking.

They must be doing a sweep round, she thought, and she'd get trapped in the middle. *How do you explain what you're doing here?*

She looked beyond her current position. There was an overgrown garden leading out to a hedge at the back, but by the time she ran there, she would be seen. Kirsten made a split-second decision not to follow that path. Instead, she turned, looked at the drainpipe in front of her, running down from the upstairs bathroom, and quickly grabbed hold of it. It would have to bear her weight because if not, she would have to shoot her way out. She shimmied as quickly as she could, with her hands on the drainpipe, and two feet on the wall, scrambling up. At the very top, she saw the bathroom window from the upstairs flat and was able to put a foot on the window ledge, before reaching up to the flat roof above.

With two hands, she grabbed hold of the edge, pulled with everything she had, and flung herself up onto the roof, rolling onto her back while trying not to breathe heavily. She took out a small mirror from her jacket, pushed it very delicately over the edge, and looked down to see the two men cross beneath her. She then rolled to the front of the building, staying low, and again used the mirror to see down below. There must've been at least eight men who got into vehicles to drive off. Kirsten breathed a sigh of relief, but knew she needed to get moving, for the drive out to the fun park would take over half an hour.

Watching them drive off, she evaluated the situation. To get her own car would take five minutes and then she'd have to play catch up. Kirsten stood up, ran across the roof to the drainpipe, and scurried back down it until she got to the ground floor. She crept across the back garden, down low, leaping through neighbour's hedges and gardens before coming out up the road. Kirsten began to run for her car.

The day was warm, the sun beating down and she began to sweat furiously inside her leather jacket. She passed a man out for a walk with his dog. He stood and watched her as she ran past before he shouted, 'Never heard of a bike for a girl?'

Kirsten ignored the taunt, instead, sliding into her car and driving off at pace. The fun park she was heading for had been built many years before and it had rapidly expanded, too. The issue with it was that it was large, and she no longer had the tracker. She'd have to scan for Johann Stein amongst a myriad of people. With this weather, many families would be out. The last thing they needed was another bloodbath like the Inverness shopping centre.

Having been there with her brother many years before, she knew there was a wooded area, a large path, and a folk-type museum with working tools from yesteryear. She also thought there was a new water section there, but she hadn't been recently.

Kirsten drove hard through the traffic, which was building up on the edge of the town as she headed towards the A9 to go south. As she climbed the steep slope up from Inverness, she wondered just what she was getting herself in for and again began to think about what Anna Hunt had said. No contact, on a kill order if she couldn't bring the man in. If she had a team, it'd be much easier. She could've scanned the crowd. This didn't seem right to go out solo-handed, to be the one amongst many, especially when there'd been such a firefight.

Part of Kirsten thought it was her guile that Anna was leaning into, but another part of her dismissed that egotistical idea. Anna was good at using people when it suited her agenda. One thing she learned about the service was it could be brutal when it wanted to.

Kirsten put her foot down on the accelerator, climbing the hill, overtaking several cars as she did so. She couldn't see any of the vans that had pulled away from the flat. She'd need to get her move on if Johann Stein was not to be taken away or have something far worse happen to him.

Chapter 08

Kirsten pulled up to the car park that was brimming with families all ready to experience the fun park. Delgado's was an attraction that'd been building for years, but Kirsten hadn't realised it had gotten this big. Instead of sitting in the queue, she parked the car up at the earliest convenient spot she could find, locked it, and walked as quickly as she could to the front desk.

The queue to get in must have been nearly one hundred people deep so Kirsten ignored them and walked off around the large thin fence that enclosed the front park area. As she got away from the crowd and into some dense vegetation, she took a step back before running at the fence, jumping, and flinging her hands to the top of it. She hauled herself over, dropping down on the other side, and quickly scanned her surroundings. She was amongst some green foliage and walked out until she could find one of the paths. A child looked at her strangely as she strode form the bushes, and Kirsten gave her a smile back.

'Did you need a wee?' the child asked. 'My mum takes me into places like that when I need a wee.'

Kirsten continued to smile and hoped that the child hadn't

been in there recently. Some distance along from the main entrance, Kirsten looked around her, and could see the woodland trail off to her left. Ahead of her was a ropes course, and beyond that, a fun park. The folk museum was further away still, but on the right-hand side was a large number of water rides.

There wasn't a pool, but water came down tubes and people were riding inside inflatables inside the tubes, sometimes three or four in each one. There must have been an underground reservoir supporting the rides.

Kirsten ignored it, instead heading off on the woodland trail trying to keep as much as possible with a crowd. She wanted to look like an ordinary tourist, so she took her gun, placing it inside her jacket before taking the jacket off and wrapping it around her waist.

The day was blistering, the sweat beginning to pour off her, and the idea of walking around with a jacket on would look so obvious. She walked over to one of the stalls, bought an ice cream and began to walk along licking it. She wondered if she smelt, as she'd been in that annoying flat for such a long period of time and while she tried to wash herself with cold water, it wasn't like having a shower. There'd been no soap either. Her hair was sticky, but she needed to keep her focus on what she was doing.

As she walked down on the woodland pass, she noticed how it rose up on a large wooden frame, the vegetation down below her as she climbed up into treetops. All around her were families with push chairs, little kids running here and there, older teenagers, some of whom look bored, headphones on their ears, and mums and dads desperately keeping everybody on the move. There were cries from babies too hot in the sun, lotion being put on the legs of little ones and shouts of 'keep that bloody hat on' from the occasional father.

Kirsten looked around, but she couldn't see Johann Stein. How would he be dressed? Would he be blending in? But there was a bigger question. Why was he here? Was he trying to meet someone? Was there a crew ready for him? Kirsten continued walking along the path, high up in the trees, and it began to double back on itself. She looked across to see a woman with a child and a man brushed past her. The woman, at the same time, went to move around to the front of the buggy causing the man to stumble. He was rough in how he got up, pushing down on the woman and then he glanced across at Kirsten.

In her short experience, Kirsten knew when someone was watching her. Like everyone, she got cursory glances. Sometimes, the odd man may even have stared at her, liking what he saw, but there was a different look, the look of a person tailing you, wanting to make sure that you didn't go out of sight. The man who had just stumbled was giving one of those looks.

Kirsten nonchalantly placed the last of her ice cream into her mouth, chewing on it as if nothing had happened, but she knew now she was being tailed. As she approached the end of the woodland path, she could see a number of figures up ahead, men who had been in the flat below.

There were no large guns, but she had to believe somewhere inside their clothing, they were packing a bullet for her. She realised now they had spotted her earlier. Whether it'd been upstairs in the flat or had it been at Ross's, when she went and met Ross, had they noticed her tailing them. Was it when she'd gone away for food? None of it mattered. They were onto her, and this was a group of people who may have opened fire in a crowded place, killing civilians at the Inverness shopping centre. It would be hard to get away.

As she drew closer to them, Kirsten spotted an older man. He seemed to be on his own. She made a beeline for him, flung her arms around him and kissed him on the lips. When she broke off, she whispered in his ear, 'I've got someone after me; I think he's a pervert. Pretend you're my husband.'

The man looked at her, almost a little too strangely at first, but Kirsten took his arm, wrapped it around her waist and walked off laughing. The man gave her a slight nod and laughed back. 'It's just for a moment,' said Kirsten, 'Don't worry. You're not married, are you?'

'Widow,' said the man. 'If I can help, it's not a problem.'

'Well, stay with me,' she said. 'Keep walking.' Kirsten took them on the woodland path past the ropes course and out towards where the water rides were located. As she got close to them, she stopped, gave the man another kiss on the cheek and thanked him.

'What's your name?' he asked.

'Susan,' said Kirsten.

'If you get any more trouble, Susan,' said the man, 'please, I'm here to help.'

'Thank you,' she said, 'but I'm going to go over there, to stand beside one of the assistants. If he comes after me from there, I'll be able to get them to radio for some help, but thank you.'

Kirsten turned and thought she caught a smile from the man before she half-ran over to the queue that was forming for the water rides.

There were four rides all originating from a large structure where a crowd was queued up steps towards the top of it. With the number of people there, Kirsten thought it was an opportunity to look down on the crowd and see just what numbers she was up against. If they came for her going up that queue, there were lots of people to get in the way. The bloodshed would be horrendous, but they would also struggle to get away.

They must have been wanting to just grab her or maybe they knew they were being watched. Maybe they'd gone up in the night and found the holes, but she was gone. Maybe they couldn't find a camera left behind. Of course, they couldn't. There wasn't one. She carried it with her. Whatever way they'd come across her, they'd decided to flush her out, possibly to flush out more than her. How could they know that she was working alone? Was Johann Stein actually here? Maybe they were calling out the opposition and they didn't realise she was on her own.

Kirsten joined the queue and saw, behind her, the man who had glared at her previously with other men behind him.

'Sorry,' said, Kirsten, 'can I just get up? My boyfriend's at the top.'

It wasn't fair, she thought. She used every bit of sexual attraction she had to bypass men in the queue for she needed to get up high to spot what was going on down below. As she climbed up high, she eventually ran into a group of people who decided that she wasn't getting any further. Kirsten was almost at the top tier, and she could see down below into the queue, where the men were trying to move up but having less success. Sometimes, there was a good side to getting attention and she had blatantly played it.

Kirsten looked down at the grounds around her. She could count at least three or four of the men down below. As the queue continued to advance, she got closer and closer to the top of the ride. She looked at the frame supporting the rides, realising, to get down, she'd be wide open and exposed, and could easily be shot at. Instead, she made for what looked like the ride with the biggest dip, one that moved quickly. As she got close, the attendant asked her, would she be riding alone? A voice came from behind her. 'There's three of us, if you want to join us, love.'

Kirsten turned to see a blond twenty-year-old. 'Are you scared, love? Is that what it is? You can hang on to me if you want.'

Kirsten ignored the obviously sexist comment and let the three of them get into the inflatable raft that would take them down the ride. She clambered in behind them, but pulled her legs up tight, making sure they were free of the men in front. The attendant pushed the ride off and she gave a little laugh and a scream as it slowly made its way out.

Just as it reached the top dip, where the raft would hurtle down the water before emerging at the bottom, Kirsten let herself fall off the back. At this point, the ride was covered over, so no one would be able to see her. The men continued down below as Kirsten put her arms and her legs out, stopping herself. Straddled across the ride, she got herself up as high as possible. It wouldn't be long before she was followed. She knew that.

Kirsten approached the edge of the tunnel she was in, where the inflatables were barely out in the open before they entered the large tube. She looked up, saw her pursuers pushing forward, wondering where she'd gone. One of them got into the inflatable, barging his way forward, saying something to the attendant.

Kirsten held herself up high as one raft passed her by with a family inside. She could hear their shock as they passed by her. She looked up and saw that the raft had gone with her enemy inside. It took about thirty seconds for it to arrive and get to the drop. As the raft descended, Kirsten put an arm down, and caught the rearmost man's neck. She jumped onto the back of the raft, twisting the neck savagely. She heard a crack and then let it go.

The raft sailed down the ride before her. She was following it, holding her feet out to reduce her speed. The raft raced out of the bottom of the ride and she could hear a few laughs and screams and then a few shouts. Kirsten slid out to the bottom of the tube and could see several of the men from the flat looking at their dead colleague inside the raft.

She had her gun out and with three shots, she sent the crowd into a panic, as she dispatched the onlooking men from the flat. Suddenly, there was mass confusion, people running here and there. Kirsten dropped her weapon inside her jacket, which was still around her waist, and bolted into the vegetation at the side of the ride. It only took her ten seconds to find the perimeter wall, which she leapt at. Grabbing the top of the wall, and scrambling her feet over the top, she landed heavily on the other side, but picked herself up and began to run.

Inside would be chaos and confusion. At least, no one should get shot. After all, it wouldn't benefit them now to be caught. They had dead colleagues they needed to get out. They wouldn't catch her now; she was gone.

Kirsten ran through the car park, got into her car, and drove away quickly. Her head pounded. Her hands were shaking from what she'd done, but she was alive. Never before had she killed somebody so openly in public. Her face would be seen now. Although she hoped the pace at which she'd done it might have made things less obvious.

She drove the car back onto the A9, up towards Inverness before pulling off down a sidetrack and stopping. She gripped the wheel, her hands shaking. What the hell had Anna got her into? Why was she on her own doing this? If she had backup, they might even have been able to take out those people without such a public execution. She thought about Dom and Carrie Anne, how as a team they'd worked so well together until the last mission which they'd been lucky to survive.

Her hand reached for her phone. She was ready to call Anna Hunt, but the instruction was to be dark, call when she had news, had their target. Something bothered her. When had they seen her? When had they clocked it was her? When had they set up the scam to pull her right into the light? Had they known about her at the bar? The man had been watching her, but he'd also been looking at Ross. Yes, Kirsten had made it all about being a friend, but they didn't know that. Clearly, they didn't know where Johann Stein was either. Would they go looking for Ross for information?

Kirsten fired up the car, and spun out of the sidetrack, back onto the A9 for Inverness. She needed to get Ross out. She'd taken them to Ross. Ross was in trouble. If they tailed him, so was his partner. Kirsten punched the wheel as she drove along. *Sloppy*, she thought. *Sloppy, sloppy, sloppy*. There was no time to continue the rebuke. She had to get to Inverness and fast.

Chapter 09

Kirsten ditched the car a few streets from Alan Ross's flat and carefully approached the house on foot. She was keen not to be on the street too long with the incident that had happened at the fun park, but she needed to make sure that Alan was safe. As she rounded the corner towards the street his flat was on, she identified a number of people who looked rather suspicious.

Previously, when she'd come past his flat, the street had not been busy. Yes, there'd been the odd neighbour, but other than that, it was remarkably quiet. Now it seemed to have people marching up and down it like the circus was in town. Kirsten turned into a driveway and then hid up in some trees, watching the street. Over the course of ten minutes, the same people were coming back and forward. She looked for markers between them, little nods and nuances to indicate that they were working for the same people and they were there. Nods of the head, the tell-tale number of fingers held out as they walked past, but the more Kirsten watched, the more she believed there were at least two sides watching this building. The hairs rose in the back of Kirsten's neck because it looked like Ross was in trouble. She picked up her mobile and made a call to the flat, but it was picked up by Ross's partner, Angus.

'Hello, this is Angus.'

'Angus, it's Kirsten. Kirsten Stewart, Ross's old work partner.'

'Oh, one of Alan's partners? Oh yes, you're that girl from the police force, aren't you? The mixed martial artist? Alan was telling me about you. We met that time, didn't we?'

'Only briefly, Angus, but I need to speak to Alan. It's urgent.'

'Well, he's probably at the station now. He's making his way home on the bus. Is there something wrong? You sound quite agitated.'

'You need to sit tight, Angus. There is something wrong. I'm going to go and get Alan. I'm afraid he could be in a bit of danger. I want you to sit tight—phone nobody.'

'Have you told his boss, the Macleod fellow?'

'No, don't phone anyone. Just understand me, Angus, sit tight. I'll get Alan to speak to you as soon as I can, but I need to go find him.'

'It's all a bit strange, isn't it?'

Kirsten wondered how she should play this. The man was clearly a little bit spooked, but also wondering how genuine everything was.

'Trust me, Angus, you need to stay put, talk to no one. Sit down, watch the telly, and don't contact anyone else. I know it sounds strange, but there could be very dangerous consequences if you don't. I'm sorry I can't tell you any more.'

'Is this to do with his police work?'

'Completely,' said Kirsten, lying. 'It'll all be explained later. Just keep your head down in the flat. Sit and watch something. Do whatever you normally do in the flat, but don't leave. Do you understand me?'

'Of course, I understand you. We've had those shootings, one just happened near Carrbridge as well. It's a terrible thing, isn't it?'

Kirsten took a deep breath. The one at Carrbridge that day had been her. Yes, she'd been followed, trapped, and ready to be shot. It still didn't help when the news was probably running what she had done. She was meant to be in the service, operating quietly, but at least she was still active. When she next saw Anna Hunt, she'd have some questions for her.

Kirsten scrolled down her phone and dialled Ross's mobile number. It took a few seconds to ring and then was picked up.

'Kirsten,' he said. 'It's been a while. You pop in to see me, and then the next second, you're phoning me. I told you everything I know. Not much else I can . . .'

'Shush, Alan, I need to talk to you quickly. Are you on the bus yet?'

'Yes, I've just got on.'

'Don't get off. Whatever you do, don't get off that bus. What number is it?'

'Twenty-five. It's heading past the hospital now, down towards town.'

Kirsten thought about where she was. If she ran to her car and drove quickly, she could probably pick up the route.

'Stay on the bus.'

'Why?' asked Alan, suddenly very serious.

'Because your life might depend on it and the life of Angus, so trust me. Stay on the bus, and I'm going to come get you.'

'Understood. I'll call the boss. We could get some backup.'

'No,' said Kirsten. 'Don't call Macleod. Don't call anyone. I don't know how far this stretches.'

'But Macleod's okay. You know that.'

71

'I do,' said Kirsten. 'And that's why I don't want to drag him in. I've already dragged you into this. Now stay on the bus and look normal.'

Kirsten closed the call and casually strolled back out of the drive, around a couple of corners, and got into her car, driving it into the heart of Inverness. She found a parking space and then sauntered along until she saw a bus stop for number twenty-five. Taking out her phone, she looked up the bus timetable and realised it would be a couple of minutes before it arrived. She glanced around on the high street and saw the fancy dress shop, the one people hired party outfits from. She quickly walked inside, grabbed a blonde wig, paid for it, and walked back out, putting the wig on her head.

As she returned to the stop, she saw the bus arriving and put her thumb out to wave it down. When it pulled over, she took a quick glance through the windows and saw Ross sitting near the rear of the bus. It was reasonably full, with at least another ten people down below. Kirsten climbed on, handed over some coins, and took a ticket, simply saying 'full way' to the driver. She sat down in a seat close to the front, turning sideways and putting her feet up on it, so she was able to clock the length of the bus through the blonde hair.

She was in trouble. Between her and Ross were ten people. She watched them closely. She reckoned at least six of them were there for Ross. One guy certainly had a handgun not well concealed under a jacket. Another one watched him like a hawk. Several others could be seen working out what they were going to do. They clearly clocked the others on the bus, so maybe they weren't all from the same side.

Kirsten would love to know what was really going on, but there should only have been two sides. Why was she a third? As the bus rumbled along right through to the other side of town, Kirsten wondered how she was going to get past everyone to the back to where Ross was. She reached inside her jacket to feel several items, one of which was a small flash bang, a device that, once set off, would make an incredibly loud noise as well as send out a blinding light that would momentarily disorientate people.

But would it be enough? There were a lot of people to get past, and if only one managed to be in some sort of shape, it could be the end for her and for Ross. On the other hand, she didn't want to be too long about this. They were clearly ready to make a move soon, but it was maybe only realising that the other side was there that was holding them off. There were also at least four innocent people there, too, and there was no way Kirsten was going to allow the bloodbath to continue, certainly not to innocent victims.

She looked up ahead and saw where the driver would be beginning to accelerate soon, coming out of the city centre streets onto roads that were slightly wider.

Kirsten saw that there was a stop approximately two hundred yards ahead, and she reached up and pressed a button that made the loud ding for the driver to know that he'd be pulling over soon. However, before the stop was a set of lights. As they approached the lights, Kirsten could see them start to turn to an orange. The driver put the foot down to try and race through the intersection, and it was at that point that Kirsten stood up to move alongside him. As the bus went through the intersection, she reached across and put one hand on the wheel and the other up on the man's face, turning the wheel hard. He lost control of the bus while it raced into one of the traffic lights before crashing into the side of a building.

Kirsten was holding on tight with one hand, having caused the incident, but the other hand was inside her jacket, grabbing the flashbang and throwing it down the length of the bus. As they struck the building, she tried to cover her ears as best she could, but it didn't fully work. She was slightly disorientated from the loud crack that had filled the air, but began to charge down the bus, hoping that nobody else would be able to react.

She passed several stunned people, hands clenched to ears, thrown from side to side by the impact of the bus. She bounced off one seat but kept her feet moving, and as she saw a man get to rise, she threw out an arm, clocking him just under the chin, forcing him back into his seat. She struggled on to see Ross, hands over ears in the rear seat of the bus. Kirsten jumped past him, kicked at the emergency exit door at the rear, and watched it fly open. Her other hand then grabbed Ross. She physically dragged him with her, and together the two of them fell out the back of the bus onto the road and the intersection.

'Up Alan, up. Let's go.'

He was disorientated. Kirsten watched his legs go off in separate directions. She put two hands on him, but her head was starting to spin as well. A car pulled up alongside them. A man went to get out to remonstrate, but Kirsten kicked the car door, so his leg was trapped, and he fell back inside.

Not nice, she thought, *but I don't need a scene.* Her hand was on Ross's collar now, pulling him along, his feet kicking out from underneath. She dragged him across to the side of a building, aware that close by, a car was racing in fast. She threw Ross to the ground against the wall behind her and drew her weapon, focusing hard as she could on what was happening in front of her.

The car pulled up. A door opened, and a man stepped out,

weapon raised. He tumbled back inside the car when she hit him with two shots to the temple. She then blew out the tires on both sides of the car before turning and grabbing Ross again by the collar. This was all getting out of hand.

Now they were out of the town centre, the pair running down a residential area. Kirsten wanted to get clear as quickly as possible. She cut down a street, knowing that a church was at the far end, and took a hard left across a garden, pulling Ross behind her. As she cornered a house, she tucked him in again behind her, and peered out, looking down the street. At the far end, she saw two men rounding the corner, openly brandishing weapons.

Damn it, she thought and turned to grab Ross and pulled him on into the church grounds. One of the problems of the grounds was that the space was open except for a few trees and headstones, and Kirsten continued to run with Ross until they got to a particularly large headstone, which she left him behind.

'Don't move,' she said. 'Whatever you do, don't move. I'll protect you, Alan, but I need you to not move.'

She saw his panicked face. He was exhausted, and maybe his ears were still ringing; she was unsure. Not many people outside of the forces were used to flashbangs or knew what to do when one erupted. If you were quick enough, and if you got your eyes closed at the right time and your ears covered before it went off, the effects were nowhere near as bad as having it come at you as a surprise. It looked like Ross had taken the full force, along with many others in that bus.

Kirsten stole off to the side of the church, a weapon in her hand, back flat up against the wall, and tried to control her breathing. Inside her leather jacket, she was sweating, but things were a little bit more out of control than she'd wanted. She suspected that she could have intercepted Ross, put him in a safe house, and then gone back and extracted Angus. Getting Angus could have been done at night, although now, it seemed that it was more pertinent to get to him quicker. They might use Angus to get to Ross, take him as hostage. The saving grace now was there seemed to be two parties after them, and the two parties were being cautious about how quickly they acted in front of each other.

Kirsten heard Ross cough, and then he pitched forward from behind the tombstone, choking somewhat and spitting out on the ground. He was probably feeling sick from the disorientation and then the run that she'd just taken him on. She heard the men shout something in Russian and come over. She waited, estimating where they had been from the sound of the voices. If they were coming at full tilt, they'd only be a few metres away. If they were more cautious, any shot may be a good fifteen to twenty metres.

Kirsten spun around the corner, saw the first man and tagged him straight to the head. The second was already raising his gun, but she caught him in the shoulder, and he fell to the ground. She didn't wait, instead running over and grabbing Ross. He was still spitting out globules on the ground. She raced to the back of the churchyard, through a small gate, down an alley, and onto another road. As she stepped out, she saw a bus coming the other way and instantly put her hand out, waving, and then took her gun from behind Ross's back and slipped it inside her jacket. As she clambered on board, she pushed Ross in front of her, and the driver gave her a little look.

'He's not going drinking in the daytime again, I'll tell you that.'

'He'd better not be sick on my bus.' said the man.

'He won't be. Don't worry.'

'Where are you going?'

'Centre. Just into the town centre,' said Kirsten. If they were lucky, the bus would get past where all the melodrama had happened. She watched as it trundled along the road before then taking a left-hand turn away from the area they'd been, and where she'd crashed the other bus. It took a slightly circuitous route before it got close to the town centre again.

She went up to see the driver, who announced to her that there seemed to be some sort of holdup in town, though he wasn't sure what it was about.

'We'll get out here, then. I think if I leave him on the bus, he might be sick,' said Kirsten.

'Good idea,' said the driver with not a lot of heart behind it. Ross walked off the bus, still clearly shell-shocked, and by the time Kirsten had got him to her car, he was still struggling to recover.

'It's all right, Alan,' she said. 'You're safe. I just need to go and get Angus now.'

Chapter 10

Kirsten deposited Ross at a safe house on the outskirts of Inverness, one that only she knew about. She knew she had to get to somewhere different from the address where she'd received the package because now, she was worrying about whose side she was playing for or indeed how many sides were playing at all. Kirsten wasn't sure why Anna Hunt hadn't given her more information, hadn't told her that her own side were there. She could have warned Kirsten that she was running into a trap. She also thought that she really didn't understand why Johann Stein was being pursued.

There was the story that he knew secrets, but it made no sense. He was still here for some reason when he should have fled the country. Everything was very confused. What she did know was now that she had Ross at the safe house, she needed to go and get his partner, Angus. There would be several people after him lurking around the house so she needed to think about what she was going to do. She gave a call to Angus and allowed Ross to speak to him briefly. The last thing she wanted was Angus being too worried; he needed to look natural when he left the flat. Not an easy task under the circumstances.

Ross was in a bit of a mess and would need some time just to calm down. It wasn't like he hadn't been in the wars before; the man had been shot once, but what he hadn't had was such crazy incidents as they'd just gone through. Kirsten wondered if any of the teams she previously worked for were aware of what her life really involved now.

When she took the phone from Ross, she explained to Angus that he was going to the supermarket. He would go in with just a bag and he would visit the one that was out by the industrial estate. Once inside, he would go through the aisles as normal, pick up a few items in the basket and then linger somewhere near the milk section. This was because Kirsten understood the layout of the supermarket. Her plan was to go in from the rear of the shop, where they held their chill store, to snatch Angus out through the back of the shop and into a car. From there she would drive off, get clear and make sure they weren't being followed, before depositing him in the safe house with Ross.

She told Angus to wait an hour before setting off. This was to allow her time to get down to the supermarket first, and make sure there was no one preventing her scheme, and also to pick up some shopping.

When Kirsten arrived at the supermarket, she no longer had her brunette hair, or indeed the blonde wig. Now her hair was red, having put on a wig from the safehouse. She changed her clothes as well. Walking in a summer's dress, she strolled casually around the shop, picking up various items such as milk and bread, butter and everything that would involve a staple diet. She picked up several frozen meals as well.

When she came to the checkout, she clocked who was working in the store and how many people, but so far, she couldn't see anyone who seemed to be impersonating staff. This was important because when Angus arrived, she should hopefully be able to tell the difference between staff and any newcomers who were on the hunt for him.

Having parked the car up at the rear of the supermarket with the groceries in the back, Kirsten started walking towards the flat, which was less than half a mile away. As she got closer, she picked up the phone and told Angus to leave and to make for the supermarket. As she passed by the flat, she was impressed, for he came down, locked the door, and turned with a wicker basket in his hand, embracing the day as if nothing was wrong. Kirsten strolled along some distance behind him, and she could see others starting to migrate in that direction. Sure, they would turn off onto other streets, but suddenly the same people were back again some four hundred yards later.

She watched Angus into the supermarket, and the others following, before Kirsten routed to the rear of the supermarket and entered the cold store. There were various people working so she grabbed a coat with the store name on it. There was a hairnet as well with which she put on over her wig before grabbing a trolley and pushing it out onto the shop floor. It contained some milk and when she got out, she started to load it onto the shelves, hoping that nobody would notice her for a while.

She clocked Angus coming out of one of the aisles, his basket now almost full and he slowly began to edge towards the milk section. There was a man behind him now moving in close, but Kirsten also saw a second man. Casually, she continued to load up the milk as if she had only one job in the world, to make sure that the shelves were stacked. From the corner of her eye, she watched Angus approach and could see the man behind him beginning to make a move. Kirsten meant to reach inside her dress for a weapon, but the second man was now pacing quickly towards them.

The man who was at the rear plunged a knife into the back of the first man. A hand went over the knife, and he began to drop. Kirsten put on a face of horror and the man who had knifed his competitor now stepped past to reach for Angus, assuming that Kirsten was just a shocked bystander. As the man's hand got close to Angus, Kirsten leapt forward and drove a kick to the man's head. She followed it up by jumping onto him as he fell and punching him three times in the face. She then turned and began to shove Angus out through the rear door of the store into the cold room area.

As she did so, a trolley came through catching Angus in the face and he spun around, blood pouring from his nose. Kirsten shoved the trolley out of the way, clocked the face of the individual and recognised him from earlier on as a worker. She ignored him and hauled Angus through to the rear of the store.

Standing in front of her was a woman in a white coat, the supermarket brand name was across her breast and she had a hairnet on. She gave a horrified look asking what they were doing, and Kirsten pulled her gun holding it up to Angus' head and advising that she was getting out of there. The woman stepped to one side, hands up.

'Of course, go. Don't shoot me, don't shoot me,' the woman said, terrified to the core. Kirsten pushed Angus past and then planted a fist straight into the face of the woman causing her to fall to the ground. She wasn't part of the staff from earlier. Kirsten ripped off the coat she was wearing, threw the hair net down, and put her hands on Angus's shoulder.

'It's me, Kirsten. Alan's friend. Onward, go.'

She pushed the man forward only to see another trolley being pushed at her. She dragged him out of the way, throwing herself flat to the wall as the trolley went past, but directly behind the trolley was a man who reached out. He grabbed Kirsten's gun hand, smacking her wrist off the wall, causing the gun to drop. He then planted a fist into Kirsten's stomach once, then twice, and reached up to grab her head before he tried to drive his knee up into her face.

Kirsten managed to get her elbows tucked in tight, blocking the knee that came up, and leaned forward, driving the man back to the far wall. He hit it with a thud but was holding her head tight. She spun with him, drove him back against the next wall, which caused him to break his hold. As soon as he did so, she reared back, grabbing his head with her hands, and showed him how to do a knee properly, pulling his head down and knocking the man out cold.

She turned and grabbed her weapon, spinning around to see someone else pointing a gun at Angus. There was no hesitation, but her shot clipped the man's shoulder, spinning him backwards, but at least taking his gun from his hand. She heard him cry out, it was in English. Good English. You might be Russian and be able to fake an accent, but not in extremes like this. Kirsten stood up and grabbed Angus, pushing him forward to the rear door. From her left-hand side, a woman approached. *Staff,* she thought, *saw her earlier. Man to the right—staff.*

'Just get down. Get down. You won't be hurt. Get down. I won't touch you.'

She watched both staff members drop to the ground, going down flat. At least they had sense. The last thing she needed was a have-a-go hero.

Kirsten pushed Angus out to the rear and saw a car pull up. The window was rolling down, but she swore she saw a high-powered rifle inside. She spun on her heel grabbing Angus with her, pushing him back inside the shop. Someone was in front of her. She caught a glimpse of the face, her mind racing. *No, staff,￼* she thought, and simply punched him hard in the chin. The man reeled backwards onto the floor.

She pushed Angus to the side, pressing down a corridor with offices on the side. She marched him forward. She turned around several times, looking back down the corridor. A man spun around the corner. Within the split second it took Kirsten to identify he was not in the shop earlier, she dispatched her weapon and he tumbled to the floor. This was getting messy. Everything was getting messy. Angus was beginning to shake.

'Get us out of here,' he said. 'You need to get us out of here.'

'I'm working on it. Just stay calm. Follow my lead. Just stay calm.' Kirsten pushed him inside an office where a manager spun on his seat.

'Sit there. Shut up!' said Kirsten, pointing her gun at him. The man raised his hands. 'No, down under the table. Whatever happens, don't move. I don't want you caught up in this.'

The man didn't take a second to react, going down on his knees and climbing under the table. Kirsten could swear he had wet himself as well.

'Angus, open that window.'

In the far corner was a window about three feet wide. Kirsten knew she had to get out of the building as quick as possible. The other sides were at the back door. They'd come in through the front. The last thing she wanted to do was try and shoot her way out. She was one gun; they were many. The whole plan was to be quick, to take Angus out the route that nobody else had thought of. It was a gamble but surely would work better than having gone to the front.

Kirsten turned and locked the door of the office before taking a cabinet and pushing it up against the inset window of the door. She instructed Angus to jump out of the other window, knowing that if he went first, at least they wouldn't shoot. After all, he was the reason they were there. If she'd gone first and not being able to survey the lay of the land, they could take her out.

As Angus hit the ground outside, Kirsten shouted to him, 'Can you see anyone?'

'No,' he said. Kirsten jumped up to the window, threw herself through and on landing scanned the area quickly. Her car was around the back but so was the other car, the one with the high-powered rifle. She led Angus over to a small wall that surrounded the perimeter of the shop.

'Down!' she said. 'Low as you can.'

In the distance, she could hear sirens. *Great*, she thought. *Police are on their way now as well. This could just get crazy.* As she watched, a lorry was coming towards them, but she could see it indicating left. This would take it along the back of the supermarket, possibly up to one of the other units that was on the estate.

Kirsten grabbed Angus, crossed the road, and ran as quick as she could until she was behind that lorry. She maintained the lorry in front of her, always keeping it between her and the supermarket as together, the two of them legged it down the road.

She saw her car up ahead. As they got closer, Kirsten

unlocked it with her key, telling Angus to get inside.

'Get down,' she said. 'Whatever you do, get down.' She opened the rear door, grabbed her dress, and pulled it up over her head. From inside she grabbed a T-shirt. The red wig had fallen off. Now she was back to a T-shirt and brunette hair and stepped into the front of the car in only her pants. There was no time to be slow about this. She started the car and drove off, telling Angus to keep his head down. She raced to the outskirts of Inverness with several police cars passing her going the opposite direction.

On reaching the edge of Inverness, Kirsten took the road out to the safe house, but she could hear sobbing in the back. 'Just stay down, Angus,' she said. 'I know it's a shock, but just stay down. I've got you. You'll be with Alan in a minute.'

Kirsten drove down the track of the safe house, a small cottage with trees around it, sheltered from view. She got to the garage beside it, opened the doors, drove the car inside, and parked up. She then grabbed everything from inside the car, including Angus, and quickly stole across to the front door. She opened it up and let Angus walk through to the living room, closing the door behind her.

Ross appeared at the door of the lounge and saw his partner. The two men ran up together and embraced, and Angus wept in the man's shoulder. It was only thirty seconds later that Ross looked at Kirsten. 'You didn't actually rescue him like that, did you?' he said.

'Every superhero wears pants,' she said. 'I just forgot my tights.'

Angus turned and looked at her and suddenly began to laugh. It was a crazy laugh, and the joke wasn't that funny. But it was letting out the tension, bringing the man back to some sort of grounding. Kirsten breathed a sigh of relief. She had Alan and she had his partner. Now she needed to work out what was going on. It was time to get back on the offensive.

Chapter 11

Now installed in the safe house and knowing that Ross and his partner would have to be kept out of the way, at least for a week or so, Kirsten decided to put her former colleague to work. Back in the days of working on the murder squad, Ross was one of the best at searching through data, easily finding it online here or there and drawing conclusions from it. She hoped he would again.

She set her laptop up in front of him and asked him to use his resources to find out where Johann Stein was. There was little to go on, but Ross could get a hold of what little government records there was on the man and start there. She watched as Angus stood by his side. Kirsten decided to give them a bit of space, took herself off to the shower upstairs and let the warm water soak over her.

She stood in the shower, looking down at her feet as images of what she'd just been through flashed by her. In the supermarket, she had clocked the right faces, hadn't she? She'd been in before; that was the purpose. Sometimes you had to trust your skills and abilities in this particular game, but that didn't stop you afterwards sitting and wondering exactly what you'd achieved or what you'd actually done. Kirsten knew she was good, knew she'd been well trained, but everybody made mistakes at some point or other. She hoped she hadn't made a bad one this time, hoped she hadn't killed anybody innocent.

The other thing that Kirsten made sure of was to have Ross call into Macleod to advise him he'd gone off sick and wouldn't be in for a while. She had to keep the distance between the team and Ross, hopefully not drag them into a world they weren't familiar with. Ross was also now under wraps. No one knew about this house. She'd bought it herself, albeit with finances that had come from the service, but they had advised her to buy it on her own. She had used a separate name, one that she'd gotten documents from someone outside the service, so she was pretty well convinced that she couldn't be found. Certainly, the Russians wouldn't get to her. Whether or not the service would come knocking, she was doubtful.

Kirsten stepped out of the shower, took a towel and rubbed down her back. She then rubbed her front and dried her legs before throwing the towel over onto a simple wooden chair. She grabbed her T-shirt, pulling it on over her because sometimes she felt self-conscious standing in next to nothing. For a moment she stood perfectly still, breathing in deeply, trying to let the stress and tension of the day seep out. She wasn't into Pilates or any yoga, but she knew the value of standing still, even if it was just for a few minutes.

Having purged herself, she dressed fully, and returned back down the stairs to Ross and Angus in the front room. So far Ross had come up with nothing, but to be fair, he'd only been at it for twenty minutes. Kirsten could see that Ross was also getting annoyed with Angus because the man was hanging on his arm, firing questions at him about what was going on. Deciding to give her man a better chance of completing his job, she asked Angus to join her in the kitchen, setting him to task preparing some food. While he did so, she instructed him on how he was to behave while here.

'Alan's got a lot of work to do. I need him on this one and you need to allow him room to work. I know you're anxious. You won't have seen anything like this, but things like these you have to let happen. Try to relax as best you can.'

'Relax?' said Angus. 'How am I meant to relax? You saw what happened today. Any of them could have shot me. I could have . . . '

'They could have shot me as well. We did well. We got out of the window because my original idea had gone to pot. The key thing is you're out.'

'But that man,' said Angus, stirring some eggs, scrambling them inside a pot. 'That man, he could have worked for them.'

'No, he didn't,' said Kirsten, a lot more authoritatively than she had been in the shower. 'Before you were there, I had gone in and got this shopping. I clocked who the employees were because I thought something like that might happen. That's why I didn't hesitate. Do you remember the other man I just pushed aside? I told the manager to get down on his knees and hide under the table. I knew who I was dealing with, Angus. I prepared myself for it. It's what I do. You have to understand that I don't work on the hoof. Generally, I'm very prepared.'

'But they might come for us here,' said Angus. 'How are we safe here?'

'Nobody knows I have this place. Nobody has seen it. I've dropped by every month or so, made sure everything's tidy and in order, and then I disappear from it. I don't usually drive here. I usually walk in from a distance. It's all part of the job, maintaining my cover.'

'Your people will know about this place, won't they? If your people know, other people could find out.'

'No,' said Kirsten, 'nobody knows about this place, and we're keeping Alan off work until I get this resolved. That means that you and Alan stay safe. It means that his boss, Inspector Macleod, Detective Sergeant McGrath and the other sergeant working with him, all are safe. I need to work out what's going on and I need Alan's help with it. I know you're scared, I know you're worried, but you need to work with us.'

The man nodded and looked down into the eggs, which Kirsten was sure had been stirred to death. 'Did you put any toast in yet?' she asked.

The man looked down. 'Blast,' he said, picked up some bread and popped it into the toaster.

'It's okay,' said Kirsten, 'but relax. Just relax. I'm one of the good guys.'

'He always said that about you. You know he was sad the day you walked. You joined this other stuff.'

'He's a big softie at heart,' said Kirsten.

'No, he's not a softie,' said Angus. 'He considers his friendships to run deep. Don't let anything happen to him.'

Kirsten nodded and then sitting, had her eggs on toast with Angus while Ross worked in the front room. After she'd left him alone for an hour or so, Kirsten came back in and could tell from the smile on his face that something had come up.

'There's not much on this Stein person. I managed to get some very basic details about him. There's an official title—said to be an advisor on the nuclear arsenal and deployment abilities, but I'm not sure that's what he does. I've never seen him noted anywhere, giving any advice. If that's what he does, he's kept very low key. He's either very good at it, and people hang onto him or he's very bad at it and doesn't do that at all. I can't confirm which he is.

The other thing to note is that the only trace I can get of him is to a holiday house in Oban. Seems he has one there, but it's let out annually. The rest of his financial records are here and there, and don't give any repetitive patterns. Yet at this holiday house, every year there's a let to a certain Georgina Rogers. Rest of the year there's no pattern. Seems like they go to whoever.'

'So, he's got a repeat customer, that's interesting, in his little holiday chalet in Oban. Don't see how that's anything to be chased up?'

Ross looked at her with a glint in his eye. 'Because the occupant is a certain Georgina Rogers. She lives in Oban.'

Kirsten raised an eyebrow at him. 'Does she now? Why would you take up a holiday let for Oban every year?'

'Unless she just likes some time away from the kids, although I can't confirm she's got any.'

'Unless she's got somebody on the side,' said Kirsten. 'Something's going on. I think I need to pay a visit. Is there anything else you can get?'

'No, he's clean in his affairs, although I think there may have been a tidy-up of files. It looks like it; traces of things having been erased.'

'Well, it was said that he had secrets for a nuclear arsenal and understanding of deployment abilities. If he's gone AWOL and they think he's defecting, to start removing stuff about him seems a fair idea.'

'Maybe so,' said Ross, 'but it may also be to simply help him disappear. What's your business with him anyway?'

Kirsten stopped for a moment and thought. Should she let

Ross into this, it would it be putting him in more jeopardy. On the other hand, he was now sitting with her. Unless she could resolve this smoothly, who knew where it was ending?

'Basically,' said Kirsten, 'I've been advised he's on the run, looking to defect to the Russians.'

'Is that what you do these days, hunt down people?'

'In a manner of speaking. I usually protect people though; we have assassins for kill orders. I've been tasked with bringing him in.'

'Just bringing him in?' said Ross.

Kirsten realised he could read her face. 'No, Alan. They've said if I can't get him in, I have to dispatch him.'

Ross looked at the floor for a moment then back up at her. 'Are you okay with that?'

'No,' she said. 'When people put a gun in my face or attack me, I have no problem with shooting back, but to take him out in cold blood from a distance . . . I'm also not convinced he is what they say he is.'

Ross sat back. 'In that case, we're in a whole load of trouble, aren't we? You're going to have to get to the bottom of this. You could tell the boss, to bring him in on it. I'm sure he could run some errands for you.'

'No, and I don't think Macleod would appreciate the idea of me getting him to run errands for me. Look, it's getting late. I'm going to go and investigate Mrs Georgina Rogers down in Oban. I will set off in an hour, so by the time I get down, it's going to be dark. Hopefully I'll find out more about her though I may be away a day or two, Alan. You need to keep Angus here. The two of you need to keep inside the house; don't go outside. You want some fresh air, roll the window down. This house constantly looks like it's locked up. Let it look like that. If you see anybody coming up the driveway, you contact me.'

Kirsten waved her hand and Alan stood up and followed her. She went out into the hall and then pulled up the carpet, grabbing a small metal panel. It opened up to large space down below. You couldn't stand up in it, but there was food stashed away with water.

'You hide here,' said Kirsten. 'You hide here, and I will come and get you. Do not take anybody on. You're not dealing with some random people, and I don't want to lose you, Alan. I'm sure Angus feels the same.'

'I actually feel the same as well,' said Ross. 'Do watch your back, too, although these days you seem to be able to look after it better than I ever saw you do.'

Kirsten stepped forward and put her arms around him, pulling him close. 'It's good to see you again, Alan. I do miss it, the old team. It's not the same working in the service. Sure, I probably save more lives, but it's not the same.'

'Well, the boss misses you as well. I don't think he's been quite the same since you left, and as for the woman he got in to replace you—drives him nuts.'

Kirsten laughed, and then climbed up the stairs to get changed into something more comfortable for driving. She packed her bag, not knowing if she'd have to infiltrate anywhere, or possibly break into a house. Once she was packed, she said her farewells, threw the bag in the boot, and started the drive from the outskirts of Inverness down to Oban.

Kirsten arrived at the address given to her by Ross for Georgina Rogers. She wasn't at a holiday house; instead she was at her own home. Kirsten watched it from the road for a while. There were little comings and goings. At one point, she saw a man arrive. He was embraced on the doorstep by the woman before going inside. She had a couple of kids running about here and there as well. Kirsten, while she watched the house, was hoping that the woman would go out, and she could tail her on her own to ask her questions, but Georgina Rogers stayed inside for the whole evening.

She let the woman go to bed before she donned her black garb and approached the house. There was no alarm functioning, so opening the door and getting inside was easy. Kirsten tore through family albums, pictures of a domestic setting, and thought the woman looked like any other mother—working hard, bringing up kids, proud to a large degree of what she was doing with them.

At two in the morning, Kirsten crept up the stairs, saw the bedroom with Georgina and her husband lying back-to-back. She checked on the kids. Everything looked normal, happy family life. Why was this woman hiring a holiday house in Oban? Looking at the address for the holiday house, Kirsten thought it was no more than half a mile away. She'd have to intercept the woman the next day. Surely, she'd go out at some point. Maybe she would go to the gym, or to some club, nursery, something else. Everybody always went to something at some point, even if it was only for coffee with friends.

Kirsten lay back in the car, trying to catch as much sleep as she could, but still keeping an eye on the road in front of her. Kirsten wondered what was coming next.

Chapter 12

Kirsten watched through bleary eyes the following morning as Georgina Rogers stepped out from her house and into the small, blue hatchback sitting in the drive. Her husband had disappeared some time earlier in a large Mercedes, shortly followed by the kids on the school bus. Kirsten had slept for part of the night. Well, at least that sentry-type watch that she did. You never truly slept, and she knew at some point, all this was going to catch up on her. Part of the job was the ability to keep going even when all you wanted to do was collapse.

Over Georgina Rogers's shoulder was a large sports bag, and Kirsten noticed that the woman hadn't brushed her hair that morning. Having watched the little hatchback pull out of the drive and then disappear down the road, Kirsten quietly followed the woman, keeping some distance back until they arrived at the Oban Leisure Centre. Kirsten parked up on the far side of the carpark, watched the woman go inside, and then monitored her as she went swimming. Kirsten would have followed her, and probably accosted her in the pool, except for the fact that she had no swimming costume with her. Walking around in a sports bra and underwear probably would have got her noticed rather quickly.

Instead, Kirsten took a seat in the viewing gallery, pretending to watch some kids at the end of the pool as if they were her own, but when she saw Georgina Rogers step out of the pool after swimming some thirty lengths, she went to the changing rooms and watched as Georgina picked up her bag. The woman walked to the toilets at the far end and Kirsten followed her in. Georgina entered the first cubicle and Kirsten made sure she checked every other cubicle before taking the bag that Georgina had thrown on the floor and jamming it up against the main door.

Once Georgina had flushed the toilet and was leaving the cubicle, Kirsten grabbed her, pulling the woman over to the sinks and forcing her head down towards one where she began to run the tap.

'Johann Stein,' said Kirsten, 'I want to know everything about Johann Stein.'

'Don't. Did my husband put you up to this? Is this my husband doing this? I'll pay you more than him.'

'Why would your husband be paying me?'

'Look, I'll confess. I meet the man. I meet the man, okay? I confess. We had an affair.'

'What's the deal?' asked Kirsten, making sure that the sink plug was in and the water kept flowing.

'We just met. It was nothing. It's nothing. I can give it up if he wants me to.'

'How did you meet him?' asked Kirsten, her hands still firmly on the woman's head.

'Conference. Look, we met at a conference, and it was just I was lonely. It hasn't been good, has it? I mean, he must have told you it hasn't been good and well, Johann just . . . it was a moment of weakness.'

'A moment of weakness that ends up with you hiring a holiday house from him in Oban, down the road. Where are you hiring from him? What's that all about?'

'I told my husband, it's just that, well, I go off and I have a bit of a retreat.'

'You don't hire a house down the road for a retreat. You clear off somewhere else,' said Kirsten. 'You've got a let from him. Why?'

'Because, well, we meet up, okay? That first time, we couldn't leave it at that, so every summer for two weeks, I tell my husband I'm going on a spiritual retreat and I don't. I go in and meet up with Johann. We have two weeks together every year. It keeps me going—do you understand that? It keeps me going.'

'So, you know him well then,' said Kirsten.

'I can leave him. If my husband wants, I can leave him, okay? You don't have to be like this.'

Kirsten began to wonder what her husband was like if she thought that he could do this to her.

'I'm going to let you up slowly. You're not going to make a run for it, if you understand me, because if you do, you'll not run anywhere. I have the capacity to break any bone in your body if I choose to. So slowly, I will let you up; you understand?'

There came a nod from the woman. Kirsten gradually let the pressure go on the woman's head and she righted herself. Kirsten could still smell the chlorine off the woman and her hair was frizzy, having been under a swim cap for the previous forty minutes. However, her flustered face made her look totally distressed and Kirsten actually felt for her, not that it was going to change what she was doing.

'Please tell me you haven't got the kids.'

'Oh, I have your kids,' said Kirsten.

'You can't take them away from me. I'm their mother. You tell him that. I'm their mother. He has to leave them.'

Again, Kirsten thought this woman's relationship was obviously in more danger than she had realised. Everything had looked perfect that morning coming out of the house.

'What is it you need to know?'

'Tell me more about your Johann Stein. You met him at a conference. Which conference?'

'It was to do with emerging biological cultures. You see, back then I used to be a chemist. I was involved in things like that. To tell you the truth, it was quite dull. Johann brightened it up and we sat at the gala dinner as they called it. I looked at him and he looked at me, and well, we just wanted a bit of fun.'

'But a bit of fun turned into you renting a holiday house from him. How on earth is that nothing?'

'Have you ever picked the wrong person?' she asked. 'You ever find yourself in the wrong place? Johann was special. He still is.'

'But he only comes for two weeks,' said Kirsten. 'Is that correct?' The woman hesitated and then nodded.

'I have your kids,' said Kirsten. 'Don't lie. Is he here at the moment?'

'He's not in the holiday house,' she said, 'But he's here, he is about.'

'Why? Why is he here?'

'To see me,' said the woman. Kirsten reached forward with her forearm, driving into the woman's collarbone, lifting her almost off her feet and she crashed her into the wall behind. 'I said don't lie to me. Why is he here?'

The woman began to cry. Kirsten fought to stop herself feeling sympathy for her. The trouble was the woman kept leading her on while holding a much deeper secret, and Kirsten had to find it. Spies were trained to lie, trained to touch your heartstrings, and people like Kirsten were trained to ignore that feeling. However, if the woman was innocent, she wondered what was happening within the family to the point she was worried that the father would have run off with the kids.

'He phoned me,' said the woman; 'okay, he phoned me. He needed me to take him groceries and things. The first night he was in the holiday house, and then he disappeared.'

'Disappeared to where?' asked Kirsten.

'He's in a bunk house. It's down by a loch. He is out of the way. You see, he's scared.'

'He's scared? He's scared of what? Being found out?'

'No. No, no, no. I'm the one who's scared of being found out. He's not at all. In fact, Johann actually asked if he should he go and speak to my husband.'

'Really?' said Kirsten. 'He threatened he would speak to your husband and do what?'

'Get me out of the marriage. We can't continue. That's why we said two weeks every year. Two weeks to make things better and after six years if we were still doing it, we said that we'd do it—we'd split. The trouble is I don't know if the kids will be coming with me or not. It's kind of scary that. We should have split last year, but Johann's good. He just does what we can do. He arranged the holiday house again until he called me one day. He wanted eggs, he wanted milk, he wanted butter. He wanted everything, just to eat.'

'Why couldn't he go to the shop?' asked Kristen.

'Because he's worried,' said the woman. 'He's worried about his work.'

'What sort of work?'

'I don't know the ins and outs. I just know he's worried about it, possibly even running away from it.'

'Why? Why would he run?'

'I don't know. He doesn't talk about that side of his work because Johann's involved with . . .'

'He's involved with what?'

'The UK's defence, security, that sort of thing.'

'Why would a chemist be involved with that?' asked Kirsten.

'He's a biochemist. I'm the chemist,' she said. 'He assesses threats, he said, for them. That's all he's told me. Look, you can pester me more all you want, but I can't tell you anything else.'

Kirsten heard the door again open behind her and saw the bag preventing it from opening. She grabbed the woman and pushed her inside one of the toilet cubicles before turning and grabbing the bag. As she pulled it towards her, the door opened, and Kirsten apologised to the woman.

'Sorry I just dropped my bag. It didn't lock the door on you, did it? Sorry, I'm just using this one.'

Kirsten followed into the cubicle where she had pushed Georgina Rodgers. As soon as she was inside, she closed it behind her and placed her hand over Georgina's mouth.

'I still have your kids,' she whispered in the woman's ear and she could feel her begin to tremble again. 'Just stay quiet, and when they go, we're going to go as well.'

It seemed like an age for the woman next door to finish her business. When Kirsten heard her wash her hands, dry them, and then depart via the door, she brought Georgina out from the cubicle.

'We're going to walk to a car,' she said. 'On the way there, if you give me any reason to, I'll kill you where you stand. Do you understand me?'

The woman nodded, and just to make the point, Kirsten pulled her gun out from her jacket, putting it in the woman's face. 'I've used this plenty,' she said, and inside, Kirsten knew she wasn't lying.

'I'd better tell him I'm coming,' said the woman.

'No,' said Kirsten. 'No phone calls.'

'But if he sees I'm coming without telling him, he'll run. He'll think my husband's with me.'

'You're not phoning him,' said Kirsten. She was worried about the man running off from the phone call, disappearing before she'd even got to the site. 'When we get close, we may phone him, but not until then.'

Kirsten indicated to the woman that she had the gun inside her jacket, and slowly, the pair walked out of the sports centre and over to Kirsten's car.

As they drove out of Oban and along to the loch side, Kirsten asked how long the man had been here.

'Two weeks. Well, coming and going,' said Georgina. 'I've popped down a few times and he hasn't been there.'

He must have been in Inverness, thought Kirsten. *He's using this as a base to operate from, but why go north to Inverness?* she thought. *What is he here for?*

'Have you seen anybody else trying to reach Mr Stein?'

'No, you're the first one, but he warned me. He said you'd be coming, and you wouldn't be gentle with it.'

'No, we won't be,' said Kirsten. 'And where am I going?' The woman pointed up to a track that disappeared through a small forest before emerging out onto the loch-side. Further up, she could see a bunkhouse, a simple affair, and a man was standing outside.

'I need to ring him. I need to ring him. You see, if he sees this car, he'll run. He doesn't know I'm inside, does he?'

Kirsten thought for a moment. Then she gave a nod allowing Georgina to pick up the phone. She watched as the woman dialled the number, listened, and heard a voice on the other end say hello.

'Go, go, go,' shouted Georgina down the phone. Kirsten took a pair of handcuffs out from her jacket, snapped them on the wrist of Georgina Rogers and then handcuffed her to the steering wheel. Jumping out of the car, Kirsten ran as hard as she could down to the scene she'd just seen.

The man was running, probably as hard as he could, but Kirsten could see that he was no athlete. He ran down across the beach, up a small slope, and into a field. It took him a moment to try and get over some barbed wire, but Kirsten felt she was gaining ground the whole time. Once over the fence, the man stumbled along.

As he got to the other side of the field, Kirsten suddenly approached the barbed wire fence and hurdled it. When the man struggled over another fence, Kirsten gained her ground. As he reached the other side, she was able to jump, put a foot on top of a wooden post, and throw herself at him. He clattered to the ground, groaning, but Kirsten rolled up to her feet, walked over, and put a firm foot on his chest.

'You're not going anywhere, Mr Stein. Everybody's after you and I don't know why. Let's go have a chat back at your rather delightful bunkhouse.'

The man turned round and stared hard at Kirsten. 'Who are you? Who are you with?'

'That's for me to know,' said Kirsten.

The man shook his head, 'Thank God you're not Russian. The Russians won't let them have it. The Russians wouldn't let it happen, but your guys, you're British, yes?' Kirsten gave a nod. 'Your guys, they were there, too, yes? Why is it happening? What are they doing? Help me understand.'

'I'm not sure they do,' said Kirsten. 'More importantly, I don't either.'

With that, she put a gun in the back of the man.

'Get over to that bunkhouse. We can sit in there and discuss what's happening. Until we do, just stay schtum. We'll soon be at a place where we're able to speak properly.'

Kirsten looked around her. Sitting on the side of the loch, they were open and exposed. Somebody could watch with binoculars from miles away. 'Inside,' she said.

Chapter 13

Kirsten kept her back to the door of the bunkhouse, looking across the room at the man and woman perched on one of the beds. Georgina Rogers had one hand on Johann Stein's, and her head was hung low. Stein hadn't looked up at Kirsten since she'd brought them into the bunkhouse, and Kirsten thought she could see tears in his eyes.

Kirsten waited several minutes before popping briefly outside the bunkhouse to check if anyone else was there. When the surrounding area had no movement, she stepped back inside, ready to question the man and find out what was going on.

'You're Johann Stein?'

The man nodded. 'That's my name, but she has nothing to do with this. Please, don't take her. Don't take her away from her kids.'

'She's got my kids,' said Georgina. 'She told me she's got them.'

Stein looked up with eyes of horror at Kirsten. 'You can't do this. You don't do this sort of thing. You're clearly British service.'

'I could be a mercenary working for anyone,' offered Kirsten, wanting to keep her independence from the subject matter, and to try and find out what was really happening, 'What's so terrible that you're going to put into motion that I shouldn't fulfil my contract?'

'You don't understand the secret I have. It's terrible. It could kill millions, start wars, and finish them. You can't—you can't do this.'

'So, what, do you have information? Some sort of missile? I was told that you worked for the UK Defence, been looking at their nuclear arsenal and deployment abilities; is that right?'

The man hung his head. Georgina put her arm around him. 'You need to tell her. If it's as bad as you told me, you need to tell her.'

The man looked at the woman. 'Don't say that. She'll think you know, torture you for the information when you know nothing.'

'Then tell me the information and trust me,' said Kirsten. 'I'm all ears. I want to know what you're on about.'

'If I told you, would you believe me, or would you just carry out your orders anyway? Surely they told you why I'm so important.'

'I told you, I'm a mercenary. As far as I'm concerned, I'm taking you in. If you want any other outcome, I'm here, and I'm listening.'

'I don't work on the nuclear side of things. I'm a biochemist, and I developed an agent. One that would devastate, kill with a rapid spread. You could plant it easily in a population. Inside of a week, they'd all be dead. It's like a nuclear bomb, you understand?'

'Surely there's some deterrent against the biological weapon. It can be treated. You can put a cure on it.'

'No. There's not,' said Stein. 'I destroyed the work for that reason. Once I made it, looked at it; I thought this is too dangerous. If one side gets this, it will dominate the other side.'

'I thought you worked for the UK. I thought you'd be at peace with that. After all, they'd hold it and keep it until they needed it.'

'You have a very blinkered view of your country,' said Johann. 'With that amount of power, they'll use it. That's why your service is after me. It's why you're here, isn't it? For them?'

Kirsten wanted to take a step back. She wanted to sit down, talk to the man properly, ask him about how and why this was developed, who was involved.

'You said you destroyed it all,' said Kirsten, 'all the work, is that right?'

'The work only exists in one place, up here,' he said, tapping his head. 'Up here is everything. That's why they want it. That's why they want me.'

'In that case,' said Kirsten, 'if you're so worried about it, kill yourself.'

Georgina looked over at Kirsten, her eyes glaring. 'What sort of world is it that a man has to kill himself for doing the right thing? What sort of world would that be?'

'A safer one,' said Kirsten, 'for a start. Wouldn't it, Johann Stein?'

'You don't think I haven't considered it,' he said. 'The problem is that there remain some samples. They're at a research facility up here in the north. They don't know they're here.'

'How does no one know they're here?' asked Kirsten. 'That sounds far-fetched to me.'

'Because I packaged, and I sent them off at a time when I was still debating what was happening with the weapon I created. I sent the samples. They could work back from them. With the right people, they may be able to work out how to reproduce what I had created.'

'But there are plenty of biological weapons,' said Kirsten. 'Why is this one so unique?'

'Because of how quick it spreads. It moves through wildlife, through everything.'

'In that case,' said Kirsten, 'how are you planning on destroying what's up at this site?'

'It's not in its final form. I just need to get in, burn it, blow the place up. That would be enough. It's not going to cause any harm.'

'Where is this place?' asked Kirsten.

'Well, I'm not going to tell you, am I,' he said. 'If I tell you, you'll tell them.'

'I'm still here, though, aren't I? At the end of the day, you've already told me enough. They can search everywhere, look for your item if I'm working for them.'

The man stood up, walked over to the window of the bunkhouse. Kirsten was going to move over and stop him in case he was signalling anyone, but she believed him to be fully on his own, except for Georgina.

'Maybe you're right. Maybe I should just kill myself. Get up, destroy this, and then kill myself.'

Georgina stood up, strode over to Johann, wrapping her arms around him. 'No,' she said. 'No, you need to be away.'

'What's been the difficulty?' asked Kirsten. 'You picked up passports not that long ago. Where were you going to go?'

'Get a ship, routing somewhere down near the Antarctic.

107

Change my name, lose my hair, something like that. Go and work another quiet life somewhere.'

'They'd find you, though,' said Kirsten. 'They always do.'

Johann turned, his eyes narrowing towards her. 'I used to always do, just concerned with the mission, not bothered about the consequences. I did what I was asked, just a soldier. That's the line, isn't it?'

Kirsten was taken aback by how passionately he gave his statement to her, and inside her mind reeled. She had seen improprieties with Anna Hunt. There were rumours about Control. 'The aircraft crashed,' somebody had said. Control had been responsible for the injuries Kirsten had suffered, and Anna Hunt had stepped in and saved her. Then Control had disappeared.

It was normal for a prisoner to be held and moved around from secret site to site, especially someone of Control's standing, high up in the Russian intelligence. The rumours had been that she was put on a plane and the plane was destroyed. If it was true, it horrified Kirsten. She had taken time to come to terms with killing people in the name of defending others, but that would have been cold-blooded murder, just like her kill order. If the man wasn't going to come with her, she was to put him down, and yet he told stories of a biological device so strong and powerful it could wipe out a country in a matter of days. His analogy to the nuclear arms race was not only intriguing, but persuasive. Kirsten found herself in a quandary.

'What happened up in Inverness?' asked Kirsten.

'Don't you know? Your people were there. Your people were there along with the Russians, and on the other side, well, I don't know who, maybe Germans. I don't think it was the Americans. One of them got their hands on me inside a shop and then all the shooting started. I managed to get away, to run, get cover in all the excitement that was going on, and the TV said they left a lot of people dead. Did many innocents die?'

'Some,' said Kirsten. 'A lot of others too. People we didn't recognise, but I never got told that any were ours.'

She almost kicked herself. She was becoming too emotionally involved. Some of ours? She just told him who she worked for. More worrying, though, was that Anna Hunt took over that scene and didn't feel like she should tell Kirsten. Kirsten was beginning to think there was a lot she hadn't been told. Bring him in or take him down, that was it. No wonder. If she'd known about this biological weapon, well then, it might have been a different picture.

'This facility, I guess it's in the Inverness direction, somewhere not far from there; that's why you were up, yes?'

The man nodded. 'But I was preparing to get there, planning how to do it, and then everybody turned up. There was all the shooting and I thought I should get out of the area quickly as possible, come here, hide up again until a quieter time, and then you showed up. How did you track me?'

'Not many people know about your liaison with Mrs Rogers here. It wasn't obvious, but I put two and two together. Why does she rent a bunkhouse from you when she lives in Oban already? What would be the point, year in, year out? I didn't buy it. I didn't buy the story of just wanting to be in the same place. Something had to be going on and it made sense that it was this is where you would come to. You have somebody able to go and do the shopping. Somebody who could step outside, let you know what was happening, pick up any other passports, tickets, or whatever you needed and none of us would be any of the wiser. I got lucky. I have a man who was able to dig deep and see the connections where others don't even begin.'

'And yet you're here on your own,' said Johann. 'Nobody with you. I think this man doesn't work for your agency, does he?'

'No,' said Kirsten, 'he doesn't, but they did come looking for him and me. There were a number of different groups looking for him as well. I think he's a man who might actually be able to help us. If you're going to go into a facility and break down and destroy what's in there, well then, you're going to need to know how to get in, have somebody who can pick up schematics, especially of places that are secret, and you will need somebody to be able to go in and do that job. You won't be able to. I can tell by looking at you.'

Stein scowled, but Kirsten shook her head gently. 'Don't be like that. I'm offering you a chance here. I'm going to take you up the road, speak to my man to go and destroy the contents in this facility, then we'll decide what we'll do with you. Maybe we'll get you out of the country and on the run, or maybe I'll shoot you like I've been asked to.'

'That's the problem,' said Johann. 'They'll kill me rather than let me live anywhere else. I can't be trusted, you see. In their minds, I cannot be relied upon not to divulge my information. I'd divulge it everywhere if I could, then it becomes worthless to everyone. Except there is no cure for this device; therefore, we have to wait, but they will still test and things will still happen. They tested with nuclear, some things went wrong. They can't go wrong with this; do you understand me? That's why I need to destroy it, and then, well, if you put a bullet in my brain, you do it, but nobody else is hurt.'

Kirsten turned away for a moment because the man's logic

was sound. If she went and destroyed the biological weapon or what remained of it, and then she killed Stein, the game was over and nobody was hurt, except for Stein, obviously, and they could go home, and everything would return to the way it was. Put Stein into the mix and somebody could still get ahead in the race. Somebody could hold other countries to ransom. What was bothering her was Anna Hunt and her own country looked like they were getting involved at the front of the race.

'Say your goodbyes,' said Kirsten, 'we leave in five minutes for the North. I don't have your kids, Mrs Rogers. I've never had them. As far as I know, they're still at school. I saw you wave them off this morning as well as your husband. I won't tell him anything, because if I do, it can get traced back to Stein and I want as much distance between Mr Stein here and anyone else. If anyone comes, do not betray him, do you understand?'

The woman nodded. 'I'll do what I can,' she said, 'but they may torture me.'

'They won't come for you,' said Stein. 'Look, she knows she hasn't been followed. She's been watching. They have to go through her to find out. By the time they find out from her, I'm gone or dead. It'll be okay. Your kids will be fine. Thank you, Georgina, thank you deeply.' Stein leaned forward into the woman, kissed her several times on the cheek before she flung herself at him and they kissed much more passionately.

'I'll be outside,' said Kirsten, 'Two minutes, max.' With that, she stepped out of the door and breathed deeply. Things had just become a lot more complicated.

Chapter 14

irsten placed Johann Stein into the boot of her car before tailing Georgina Rogers back to her house. She took a tour of the area, making sure no one was watching the house before departing back alongside the Caledonian Canal to Inverness. She stopped once on the way up, pulling into a woodside glen to check on Stein in the boot. The man looked haggard, but he seemed to be reasonably comfortable, and she tried to drive at a speed and with a deftness that meant he wouldn't get bounced around in the boot.

When she reached the outskirts of Inverness, the rain had started to pour down. Kirsten made a beeline for the hidden-away safe house. She parked the car inside the small, attached garage before letting Johann Stein out of the boot, and pulled him to his feet. She held his shoulders, looking him in the eye.

'You're on probation, Mr Stein. I hope you understand that. If I find anything of what you've told me is wrong, you're going straight to the police and I'll wash my hands of you. Whatever you do now, you tell me the truth. One thing wrong and I walk, and we deliver you. If anything from our dealings hurts any of the two men that I'm about to introduce you to, I will kill you myself. Are we clear?'

Stein nodded and Kirsten led him quickly out of the garage and into the small house. As they came through the door, Ross appeared in the hallway.

'Johann Stein,' he said. 'You've brought Stein here?'

'Yes,' said Kirsten. 'Mr Stein, meet Mr Ross.' Ross stepped forward, putting a hand out in a fashion that Kirsten knew so well. The man was polite, civil at all times; despite the fact he just spotted an enormous danger in Stein being there, he still shook him by the hand. A voice shouted from the end of the hallway.

'Have we got someone else in?' It was Angus from the kitchen, and Ross shouted down the hallway.

'Two just came back, whip something up for them. They look hungry.'

Angus poked his head out of the door to the kitchen. 'Hello,' he said. 'Who's that?'

'Stein,' said Ross.

'The guy you told me everybody's looking for?'

'That's the one. He's with us now. Just in case there weren't any more people looking for us already.'

Ross opened the door to the living room and invited Stein in, and Kirsten followed.

'My hunch was right, then?' offered Ross.

'I did tell him there weren't many who could dig that deep. Well done, Alan. It's a good find, although I don't think it makes us any safer.'

'No,' said Alan. 'I imagine it wouldn't, but can I ask why he is here?'

'Mr Stein may need our help,' said Kirsten. 'What I'm about to do, I want a second take on. Frankly, you're the most

113

experienced person in the building outside of me.'

'There's only three of us apart from Mr Stein and Angus won't have any experience of this type of thing.'

'Exactly,' said Kirsten. 'I need to go with your decision. See what you say.'

'What about Anna Hunt? Why don't you just contact her?'

Kirsten shook her head, walked over to the window of the cottage, and looked out. 'Anna Hunt may be part of the problem.'

'That's not good,' said Ross. 'Okay, then, hit me with it.'

'Sit down,' Kirsten said to Johann Stein. 'Sit down and tell Mr Ross here everything you know.'

'Call me Alan,' said Ross.

'We don't need to be so civil,' said Kirsten, and she walked over and leaned in Ross's ear. 'You treat him as a hostile witness. I'm not sold on everything he's saying yet.'

Ross nodded, but turned around and smiled politely. 'It's done. Take me through from the top then,' he said.

Kirsten excused herself and went to the kitchen to make herself a coffee. Angus was still there, and Kirsten could see the worry in his face.

'Why is that man here?' he said.

'I told you why. He's coming to help. It's who we're looking for.'

'Yes, but if you found him and you've been looking for him, why isn't he going off to meet some of your other people and why am I not going home?'

'Because,' said Kirsten, 'the tale he's telling is a different one to what I've been told. Not that I've been told much. Alan's going to help me clarify which is the correct story, because if what Mr Stein's saying is true, we've got a lot more we need to do.'

'Can't we just dump him over now we've found him? I mean, that was your job, wasn't it? Wasn't it? Alan was helping you find him.'

'Yes, that was my job,' said Kirsten, *and then to kill him*, she thought. *Bring him in or put a bullet in him. Some choice!*

She remained in the kitchen, trying to assess just where Angus was in all of this, as he flittered about the kitchen. He made sandwiches and took them through to the main living room, then he came back and cooked himself an omelette.

'You need to chill out,' said Kirsten. 'You've got a TV. Put it on. No Internet attached to the TV. Everything is done through an encrypted line. It's private as well. It's not from the agency, but I don't want to overload it, so I didn't put the TV on it. We can silence it quickly then. Nobody knows who we are, because TVs pick up broadcast signals.'

'This is all to do with those shootings, though. Alan told me about what happened on the bus, getting him out. Look at what happened with me. Are we getting back out of this, Kirsten? Are we? Are Alan and I going to be able to go back to that flat?'

'I hope so,' said Kirsten, 'because I have to walk away from this as well.'

'If we know that they want him and you've got him, why not just simply hand him over?'

'Listen,' said Kirsten. 'What this man knows and is capable of doing can bring down a country. What's in his head is dangerous. So very dangerous, and that's why they want him. Everybody wants him. What I've got to work out is can I take the danger away?'

'Well, can you can clean this up?'

'To a degree,' said Kirsten. 'I've got to make a decision. Do I let Mr Stein go away, or do I have to put him away?'

Angus' face became pale. His jaw dropped. Kirsten found him staring at her. 'Are you for real?'

'Unfortunately, yes,' said Kirsten. 'These are the decisions I get to make. That's why Alan's going to help me work it out.'

When she'd heard the talking had died down from the front room, Kirsten re-entered and sat down on a small chair opposite Ross and Stein.

'Have you told him everything?' she asked Stein.

'Everything I've told you.'

Kirsten looked over at Ross. 'What d'you think?'

'What I think is that I need to check some things out. The facility is just outside Dornoch and I have contacts, ways, and means in the net to get through to it. I can probably break into certain manifests.'

Ross stood up and walked over to Kirsten, leaning down to her ear. 'His story's good, but we need to check it. I need an hour to get as much evidence as I can.'

'Take three or four,' said Kirsten. 'I'm going to bed. I haven't slept properly in however long.' Ross nodded, and Kirsten turned to Stein. 'We need to give Alan some time on his own. You, Mr Stein, can go upstairs into the small bedroom. I'm going off to my own. Just be aware, if you try to run I will shoot you and I will bring you in. At the moment you need us. You're just an extended hassle to me.'

This wasn't, of course, true. Kirsten was extremely worried about what the man had said, but she wanted to play it like she wasn't convinced yet, but she knew somewhere deep inside the fact that she'd brought him to Ross meant that she believed the man already.

Kirsten watched Stein climb the small stairs to the upstairs bedrooms. Once she was sure that he had taken himself off to bed, she found her own. She was sure that she smelled after having travelled so far in her clothes for so long, and she slipped everything off to dive under the covers. She kept her weapon, however, underneath the pillow on her bed.

As Kirsten lay in the bed, she struggled to get to sleep. She'd finally stopped, was waiting on someone else to do some work, so her mind unravelled and the first thing that came into it was Craig. She had left him in her own flat, not able to tell him what she was doing or where she was doing it. A part of her wanted to go to him now, to bring him in on this, get him involved, to get his read, but she knew if she did that, it was more than likely she'd be spotted. Anna Hunt, Godfrey, and the rest of the service knew what Craig meant to her, could see what she meant to Craig, and they'd almost expect her to run to him.

Then she got a horrible thought. *Was Craig in on it then as well?* She shook her head. No, she needed to get that away from her mind as soon as possible. After all, he'd been there for her, always about, and now it crossed her mind where she'd met him. He'd been the driver down in London when she'd been introduced to the inner circle, to Godfrey. Was that part of the ploy, that he'd been a setup? It couldn't have been.

Kirsten thought herself to be tired, but another part of her thought that was why she couldn't go to Craig. She couldn't trust him. Maybe that was because of the position he held at the moment. Or maybe trust was the wrong word. Maybe she couldn't trust him being able to hang on to the information she gave without being compromised. Ross was different. Ross was involved. He was smack in the middle of this and needed a way out. He was going to help her and he'd always been good, always been honest. Alan Ross was one of the best, and a friend, a friend who had simply come from her previous job.

It took Kirsten another twenty minutes before she fell asleep. The next sound she heard was her door opening and she took the gun from under a pillow with bleary eyes, pointing it at the door, as she sat bolt up in bed.

'It's all right, it's me,' said Ross. 'I've got some stuff for you. Stein is asleep, thought it best to come and talk now.' Kirsten was aware that the duvet had fallen down from in front of her and she was fully exposed.

'Good job wasn't somebody else,' laughed Ross, and walked out. Kirsten chortled herself. Indeed, it was. She stood up, pulled on some fresh clothing, and quickly went down the stairs. As she sat down in the seat opposite Ross, she noticed that a cup of coffee was already waiting for her. That was Alan all over. Every time he was ahead of the game, knew what you would need.

'So, what have you got for me?' she asked. 'Apart from loitering in my room.'

For a moment Ross looked a little worried and she thought he was about to apologise, but then he clocked her manner and gave a laugh.

'Well, this facility he's talking about. It's quite funny; the facility itself is not one of the well-hidden ones, which may be why he sent it there. If he was ever going to destroy the items, the last thing he needed was for them to be locked away somewhere with a lot of protection. There were three different packets sent up to it for storage, all coming from Mr Stein. That record, or at least it's from his office, that record is established. I got that when I broke into the manifest system.

Obviously, what's inside those packets I have no idea. The inventory shows it as some sort of magnesium formula, but it doesn't make any sense to me beyond that. They're also listed for possible future disposal and a redundant project. I guess he's linked it into something that he hasn't had anything to do with in a long time. It is notable that it's just come out of his office. It's not Stein directly who sent it there. He's probably been clever and got a clerk or someone to package them and post them.'

'What else have you found?'

'He has certainly been working on top-secret items, but I can't get through to work out what they are. One thing I did do was tie in the police report, at least the initial findings, with what was going on from those provided by your service about the incident in Inverness. Nobody really reads these things because they've taken over. It's almost a courtesy. At the end of the day, it usually repeats back what we've said. Except there's two bodies not there anymore.'

'Stein said some of our service people were there. Maybe that's what's happened. Anna's taken them off the record.'

'I can't say for definite,' said Ross, 'that his story is true, but certainly there's evidence that supports it. Whether that's to a degree where you're going to put your life on the line, I don't know. You have more experience in these sorts of things than me.'

'What's your gut say about him, Alan?'

'My gut says he's not lying. My gut says there's a man there who's worried, a man who doesn't know where his life's going to go, a man that's hoping against hope that you could come through for him.'

'And if it's as he says it is?'

'If there's even a chance it's as he says it is, we have to act,' said Ross. 'We have to make sure that nobody gets hold of that weapon.'

'So, I have to go and destroy these items he sent up to the other research lab?'

'Yes,' said Ross, 'and if somebody comes to take him, you'll have to put him down.'

Chapter 15

Kirsten and Ross spent the next day and a half searching for schematics of the facility they'd have to infiltrate to recover and destroy the samples that Stein had quoted. Most of the work of planning the operation was done by Kirsten, but she needed Ross's ability to hack into systems to find schematics, however old, to give her a full awareness of what she was looking at. Part of her wanted to do a recce of the area, but she decided against it, aware at the moment that many people were probably looking for her. Anna Hunt would have expected her to make contact by now at least to know where Stein was. Though she was being put out on her own, she never went dark for too long in this service.

As the second day wore on, Kirsten began to think of what weaponry she would need to infiltrate the base. Ross had found a sewer system running underneath it, and believed there was a way in, but had no idea if that route would be blocked to some degree. These sorts of facilities were not unaware of what was around them, or indeed what they were built on top of, but Stein had been clever, and he posted the items in question to a low-level facility, one that certainly wouldn't have the high security that he had worked at previously. Stein also advised what the item would look like. A simple cardboard box with numerous powders inside. As the second day was coming to a close, Kirsten decided that she would go to her hidden armoury and pick up what weaponry she required.

It was a small store close to cliffs and she believed she could approach it stealthily, leaving the car some distance away. Normally she wouldn't think twice about going there, but not understanding exactly where her own service lay, with regards to Mr Stein, and also her current actions, she didn't want to attract any undue attention. Kirsten put on her black leggings, black top and jacket, and advised the three men she was leaving behind not to venture out at all. Ross was also told to keep an eye on Stein, and because Kirsten didn't trust him fully, she handcuffed Stein to a chair for the period that she would be away, handing Ross a gun. He looked at it, almost disgusted and went to give it back, but Kirsten insisted, pushing it into his hands.

'It's for protection,' she said. 'In case he tries anything on you or Angus, you don't have to threaten him or anything. He's sat there, he's handcuffed to that chair. Don't go within two feet of him, and if he comes out of the handcuffs, shoot him.'

Kirsten made it all sound so straightforward, but to Ross, this was not how you held prisoners. They were processed through the system, got interviews which were recorded. He didn't hide out in the middle of nowhere with people, believing their story, yet treating them like the enemy.

Having made sure that the house was secure, Kirsten took the car from the garage and drove a little way further north, parking the car about half a mile from the cliff edge. From there, she disappeared into woods, moving towards the coast before climbing halfway down a cliff. Then she scanned the beach that was running along in front of her, and when satisfied that it was empty, she descended and stole along it, trying to stay up on rocks to avoid leaving footprints in the sand. After walking some six hundred metres up the beach, she turned to face the cliff edge and began to climb up. The actual cave that her stash was sitting in was not visible from either above or below, and you had to get up close to see the entrance. Once you'd pulled yourself up the cliff to the correct height, the only way in was on your belly, so small was the opening.

Kirsten checked the stash on a six-monthly basis, for this was somewhere to come to when she couldn't simply walk into the office. Having crawled some ten metres on her belly, the cave opened, and Kirsten was able to stand, smelling the damp of a flow of water that she had to slide across. She felt slightly wet on her front, but she ignored that. Walking over to a crude chest, she inputted the security code, and it flew open, revealing a number of weapons as well as other measures inside.

Kirsten picked up many flashbangs, several hand weapons, and a couple of automatic rifles. She wouldn't take any grenades and she would only shoot if she had to. The trouble with grenades, of course, were they were indiscriminate.

When a sound came from outside, Kirsten knelt down inside the cool but damp cave, focused on the entrance. As she watched, a small figure was sliding in on its belly. She recognised the dark hair and lowered her weapon, but not fully.

'You said not to check in until I had something,' said Kirsten. 'Yet here you are, arming yourself to the teeth.'

'It is quite dangerous out there. You do realise that, don't you? Shootout in the shopping centre.'

'Several people taken out at a fun park. Very public, Kirsten. We're not impressed.'

'Neither am I, but those men had to be taken out very publicly. They put me into a trap.'

'Even so, too much noise,' spat Anna. 'You know we're trying to keep this quiet.'

'I guess that one's out of the bag,' said Kirsten. 'Seems to be a lot of people after this particular subject.'

'Yet nobody can find him. You disappeared from the Inverness area.'

'Oh,' said Kirsten, 'did I? Where did I go?'

'We don't know. That's why I'm asking.'

'I was just chasing up a lead which came to nothing.'

'Where's Detective Constable Ross?'

'Safe,' said Kirsten. 'Been a number of people after him since I spoke to him.'

'I believe the only reason you could want to speak to him' said Anna Hunt, 'was to get the lowdown on what he had seen at the shopping centre, but you have my full report.'

'First-hand is always better than that report, though, isn't it?'

'You could have spoken to me,' said Anna.

'You were later on to the scene. Ross was there early.'

'Why him? Why not the officer who was running the show? Why not Macleod?'

'Ross is easier to talk to and certainly with the detail of the situation.' Kirsten wasn't lying with that; Ross would remember everything that happened. Macleod knew the fundamental details; he also knew what was important, certainly much more

124

so than Ross would. The man was like an old bull, able to go at the subject, but quite often ignoring what was happening on the periphery.

'I just thought you might have been in touch by now,' said Anna. 'You've taken two civilians to ground; we could keep them for you.'

'Have you got many outside there?' Kirsten pointed to a small hole that Anna had come in from.

'Why would I have a number of people? I've come to speak to you. I've come for an update.'

'Yet you never asked me to report in that fashion. You said when I heard something, when I had something, then report.'

'The government's getting very worried about Stein. This is a race for power, a race to get there before other nations. To make sure that he doesn't give away any of our secrets.'

'Can we drop that?' asked Kirsten. 'Can we drop the pretence?'

'How do you mean?' asked Anna.

'Stop the lies. At the moment, the man's on the run. We know he's been up in Inverness. Hopefully he's still in the area, but the last thing we need is anyone else getting injured.'

'The government's not going to wait long. We're going to have to move,' said Anna. 'I need you to come in, put you on a task force with others.'

'Why?' asked Kirsten. 'What's changed?'

'It's an arms race. We can't have any other nation having the upper hand; we cannot be threatened from elsewhere. Our nuclear threat is being supplanted.'

'So what; he's going to give away defence codes and leaks, and therefore, we're going to be weakened? Is that what you believe?'

'Exactly,' said Anna, 'that's why you need to come in.'

Kirsten shook her head. 'I don't think it's wise at the moment. Like you say, Ross is off the street. Everybody's safe.'

'You can always maintain that cover.'

Going through Kirsten's mind was the idea that she'd somehow been picked up. At some point, her car would've been identified and that's how Anna was following her, or had she done it previously? Had she been so good that she'd actually followed Kirsten in the quiet times so she knew where her stash was? Clearly, she didn't know where the house was, but Kirsten had done that one well. Anna may not even be sure that she had a secret house.

'I don't think it's wise to come in at the moment,' said Kirsten. 'I'm chasing up a lead. It might be something; it might be nothing.'

'What?' asked Anna. 'You can fill me in on it so I can pass it up the chain, keep them happy.'

'I prefer to operate in the dark, but I won't be long.' With that, Kirsten turned to leave.

'Oh, we're going, are we?' said Anna. 'I thought I was giving you a direct command.'

'You put me out here on my own; the least you can do is let me follow it through.'

'Okay,' said Anna, 'but I will need to speak to you in the next day or so. Where shall we meet?'

'I'll give you a call,' said Kirsten, with absolutely no intentions of living up to that suggestion.

'I'll go first, then,' said Anna. She backed her way out of the little hole as Kirsten lay on her belly within it. By the time Kirsten had got to the edge of it, and was looking around, she could see Anna Hunt walking away down the beach. *How had she got there? How had she got in?* Kirsten turned back to her bag, finished her last-minute packing, then flung it over her shoulder.

If she'd been waiting here, the last thing Kirsten wanted was for her to notice when she left. Kirsten thought about leaving from the front, but instead she decided to use the rear door, the one she'd never walked down before. She had cut a small tunnel, one she was going to have to crawl on her belly through, and it would go up and up until it broke out through the cliff top in the midst of a copse of trees.

Slowly, in the dark of the cave, Kirsten felt her way around and found the passage that you could barely see without a decent torch. She squeezed through it, pulling the bag behind her until it got to the point where you had to climb upwards. She then pushed the bag ahead of her, eventually breaking out into the night again. This time she was on top of the cliff three hundred metres away from the edge of it. She crept off, paralleling the beach and then stopped, searching with her infrared goggles through the night.

Anna Hunt was down on the beach. There was a large number of men with her all carrying weapons. Clearly Anna had meant not to leave her. Kirsten took an hour to get back to the car, stopping several times, checking to see if she were being watched. By the time she got into the car, and then drove on a long secure route, checking the whole time that nobody was following her, the dawn was ready to break.

As soon as she got back, she parked the car in the garage, entering the house on the stroke of five. She opened the door to the front living room and Ross was lying in the chair asleep, the gun still in his hand. Across from him, Stein was snoring, hands still cuffed to the chair.

Rather than waiting, Kirsten strode into the kitchen at the rear of the house, realising there was a light on in there. Angus was standing in front of the kettle.

'It works on its own, you do realise that, don't you?' asked Kirsten, and Angus turned round, the man's face pale white.

'How do you take this? I can't sleep, I really can't.'

'This is nothing,' said Kirsten. 'Wait until we get some real heat.'

Kirsten studied the face of Angus and realised that the man wasn't sleeping. She heard somebody paddle into the room. Looking over her shoulder, she saw Ross, his gun still inside the front room while he was hanging through the door.

'When are we going to see an end to this?' asked Ross. 'I'm not sure Angus is going to survive it.'

'I don't know,' said Kirsten, 'I just spoke to my boss, and quite frankly, I think she's lying through her teeth.'

Ross walked over to the kettle, pressed it on. 'It's not good then,' he said. 'it's not good at all.'

'You're telling me,' said Angus and shot Ross a filthy look. Ross's face looked dejected, and Angus stormed off and up the stairs.

'Go and deal with it. You're going to need each other to get through this one,' said Kirsten. 'I'll keep an eye on Stein; don't worry about me.' She waited until the kettle had boiled, the two men had departed and then came through with a black coffee, sitting down in front of Stein. Half of her began to doze, but the sentry eyes and ears picked up Stein's movement.

Stein rolled his neck, trying to wake up, stretching out his limbs, having awkwardly slept. 'Did you get what you needed?' he asked.

'Very much so. I got enough,' said Kirsten. 'And I also ran

into a little bit of heat from my boss. We move out tonight for the facility, get that destroyed, and then we'll talk about what we do with you next.'

'You get that destroyed and I don't care where I go.'

No, thought Kirsten, *but I do, because everything inside of me says it looks like a termination for you, my friend.*

Chapter 16

After her return to the house, Kirsten was having second thoughts about taking on the storage facility on her own. Part of her wanted to take Johann Stein with her because with the interference of Anna Hunt, she was worried what would happen if she left Ross and his partner on their own with Stein. Previously, she thought, she was untraced and maybe she still was, but Stein being around Ross was not a good idea. It wasn't just Anna Hunt she was worried about. If the Russians turned up as well, she was putting the two men in extreme jeopardy. It was better for her to clear out with Stein and leave Ross and his partner secreted in the house so as not to alarm them. She advised Ross that Stein would be coming with her, just in case she came across anything that warranted his previous knowledge of all the systems.

'I'm not detecting any of that when I go online. I can't find anything in the schematics that suggests that,' said Ross.

'No, but schematics don't say everything. Besides, I can keep him close. You weren't too keen the other night when I left you, not too keen to hold a gun to him.'

'You still don't trust him then?'

'You learn in this game not to trust anyone,' said Kirsten.

'The only reason I trust you is because I know you from before. We built that trust. Johann Stein hasn't earned much with me so far.'

'But he hasn't lied to you either.'

'No, but I don't know if he's been economical with the truth either. You have to keep all of your options open in this game, Alan. It's not always the most fun one to play.'

Kirsten spent the day prepping herself and sleeping before her mission that night. She also insisted that Stein get some sleep. It was ten o'clock that evening before she left in the car, saying goodbye to Ross. She advised him to stay put until she came back, and if she wasn't back early, Ross wasn't to get overexcited but simply hole up for at least a week. It was best that Kirsten give the all clear.

Ross nodded his acknowledgement, but then he hugged her and held her tight. 'Just you take good care, okay?' he said. Then he stepped back and looked at her. Had it been another bloke, Kirsten might've felt that they were scanning her figure, checking her out, but Ross wasn't interested in that.

'You've changed, haven't you?' he said. 'Much more clinical, less fresh-faced, world on your shoulders at times. I'm not sure it's for the better.'

'Well, thanks,' said Kirsten. 'Thanks for the pep talk.'

'But you are more clinical,' said Ross. 'Boss was right. You are suited to this work.'

Kirsten couldn't decide if Ross was actually being complimentary or whether he'd finally realised a defect in her. The man had just seen her take out a bus with several people who had been after Ross and he'd probably been spoken to by his partner about what happened at the supermarket. Did he now see her as someone who could kill or did he see her still as a hero, saving himself and his partner? Kirsten didn't know. Alan Ross was sometimes very hard to read, polite to the core, but his true feelings buried deep.

The facility was just over an hour away and Kirsten headed north with Stein once again in the boot. She had her balaclava beside her and was dressed fully in black with a number of weapons sitting in the back seat of the car. She didn't want them in the boot with Stein because her trust didn't go that far.

They were a little distance from the facility when Kirsten turned off the road at a small holiday park. It was late at night and most caravaners were inside, but she saw the dark one on the end. It was a temporary safe house they had, not as good as a lot of the others, but if they were in need, it was a good one to be put into. People often forgot about things like caravans.

She parked up beside it, checking no one was looking before letting Stein out of the boot and then introduced him to the delights of the caravan. She advised him he should keep the lights off, probably stay in one of the bedrooms. If he heard anything, there was a hatch in the floor to drop out and he could escape to wherever. Kirsten handed him a handgun.

'I don't know how to use it.'

'Point and shoot,' said Kirsten. 'If they're coming for you, you need to defend yourself.'

'I suppose you're right,' he said. 'It could force them to kill me. As long as you do your job, that would be everything wrapped up.'

Kirsten's eyes were sad, but she tried to give a laugh.

'I wasn't joking,' said Stein. 'It is one of the ways I see out of this.'

Kirsten nodded, wished him all the best and said she'd be

back before morning. She stepped into her car again and drove the short distance up the road before finding the outer perimeter of a government storage facility. She could see a guard patrolling, and after she parked the car, she headed off into a small wood, looking to find where the sewers ran out to the sea.

The pipe wasn't the largest and she had to crawl on her front before she entered it. She stowed her high-powered rifle and some grenades outside, taking only her two handguns, a knife and a large amount of explosive. This would be a quick infiltrate. Get in, prime the bombs, and explode them. Once it had gone up, she would race back to the caravan and hide out there.

She crawled along the pipe. She curled her nose up at the smell of it and forced herself to go up onto her elbows and knees to try and keep out of the worst of what was passing her by in the pipe. As she got closer, she suddenly had a large grill in front of her. From inside her pocket, she took out a small blowtorch and spent the next half an hour cutting through the grill, before being allowed to move farther into the complex. She was counting the distance she had travelled, struggling to get a satellite read for where she was, but it wasn't long before, with her torch, she identified the hatch that would lead upwards. The only trouble was it had been concreted over and only the handle remained sticking through.

Kirsten nearly swore, but instead she backed up, returning back down the pipe and out to its entrance. There was always the possibility that this could happen, so Kirsten had decided she would have a second route of entry. Looking inside her bag, she found the blanket that she carried with her until she got to the barbed wire fence at the rear. She threw the blanket over the fence, climbed up the wire and rolled over the top, keeping safe from the spikes. Once inside the complex, Kirsten kept low, looking for the guards that were walking the perimeter.

She pulled her blanket down, storing it in the grass, ready for her escape. There was a rear door with access and Ross had provided the code that had been current the day before. Kirsten approached, avoiding the perimeter lights that shone down, tapped in a six-digit code and breathed a sigh of relief as the door opened.

It wasn't a high-level facility, and in truth, she was pretty sure she could breeze in and out. As she entered the corridor beyond the door, she saw several doors off it, and thought she had heard a lot of noise from inside. As she stole along, she swore that the place was being inspected for she could hear a voice ahead.

'The package will have arrived some time ago. We need to know where you've put it.'

'The problem is, sir, that if you don't have the actual detail, the number, we can't find it. It will take a manual search. It could take a while.'

Somebody was on to what Kirsten already knew, that Stein posted the package to this facility. She took a breath and walked through a marked door. Somebody had labelled the storage area B, according to Ross, and that was where the package should be. Kirsten was anxious now that other people were looking for the item and they would be in the building as well, but she needed to destroy it.

She began to search long numerous racks. Everything was boxed up with just a stamp on it. It took Kirsten almost fifteen minutes to identify the box on the racks but she did so. It was at the very top, high up and looked like she would need some sort of forklift to go underneath to lift it down.

She quickly climbed up the racks, reached the top and saw the screwed down lid of the box before her. She took out a miniature drill, worked out the screws before sliding back the lid and looking inside. There were a number of jars of powders, ones that needed to be destroyed according to Johann, but there was also some hardware, what looked like some sort of delivery system, a prototype maybe.

Kirsten wasn't worried that this particular item could do damage immediately, but if it was coupled with the brain of Johann Stein, then the devious design, which could go through a country in a matter of several days, may just be able to be implemented.

Kirsten took the explosive devices from within her bag and placed them inside the casing. After setting a timer, she put the casing back on top, understanding she had five minutes to get out of the building. She re-screwed the cover, climbed down, and went to the door, ready to run along the corridor. In her head, a mental number was ticking down from three hundred. She was currently at one hundred and fifty.

As Kirsten went to open the door to get outside, she heard motion in the corridor outside and the door to the storage area swung open. Kirsten swept in behind it. Suddenly, all the lights in the room were switched on. She tried to blink quickly, adjust her eyes to the brightness, but she saw a pair of grey trousers walk past her, followed by a number of people in what seemed like janitorial outfits, dark blue lab coats. In reality, she thought they should have looked like postmen, because that's what they did here. Take the post and file it.

She crouched, watching them walk along and realised they would have less than a minute and a half before the bomb would go off. She had to do it, though, even though she wasn't sure who these people were. Kirsten decided that she had to get out, as if the devices went off and she were still in the room, there was a serious danger she could get injured. There was also the problem that everybody else would suddenly run to that point.

The men who had entered had left a guard on the door. Kirsten stood up, snuck a hand around his neck, and broke it before letting him tumble to the floor. As she stepped out of the corridor, she heard a cry and ducked as the wall behind her was suddenly peppered with bullets. She drew her gun firing off on one side, and turned right, walking backwards, down the corridor. As two men raced around the corner, she shot them dead before they could fire any weapons, and she kept walking backwards until she hit the door. Kirsten turned to hit the keypad, and punching the numbers to get out, she kept her weapon raised and firing shots down the corridor, deterring anybody else that would come around that corner. Once the door was open, she pushed it and raced through, driving it closed behind her.

She ran up towards the fence and heard cries, flinging herself to the floor as gunfire raced over the top of her. She rolled onto her back, looking for who was coming towards her, and then a loud explosion rocketed through the building. The tremor caused everyone to fall off their feet and she found the blanket she had earlier left on the ground. Picking it up, she made a wild throw, seeing it just about hang onto the fence.

Kirsten turned, fired twice, challenging those who had come after her to stay on the ground and made a jump to the fence. She scrambled hard, pumping her legs, but she was out in the open and a shot went past her too close for comfort. When she reached the top, she didn't lower herself down but simply fell, landing hard on her knee. As she stood up, it threatened to buckle, but she had her weapon out and was firing back through the fence.

Quickly, despite the pain she was feeling, she stole off into the dark. When she reached the car, she jumped inside and drove off with no headlights on. As she raced down the road, she pulled in briefly behind a tree, letting several police cars and army vehicles pass her by in the dark.

The word was out. She'd need to get to ground. Kirsten hit the main road before switching her lights on and then drove it a steady sixty miles an hour back to the caravan park. As she came close, she could see the place was an uproar. There was a police car with flashing blue lights on the side. Ambulances had turned up, and as Kirsten looked across, the caravan she'd left Johann Stein in was heavily damaged. The door was hanging off and there were a number of bullet holes in the side. She pulled her car up a little distance away and walked back. If Stein was in there, she'd have to get him out. Did the police have him or was he in an ambulance or worse still, had whoever come for him got him and was now taking him away?

Chapter 17

The scene before Kirsten was chaos. There were police cars there. Clearly, there were bodies as well. She was unsure if Johann Stein was in the middle of it. Would he be on the ground? Had they snatched him?

She needed to get close and yet the last thing she wanted to do was walk into the middle of a scene like this. There would be too many police constables able to look and remember faces—trained to do so. She stole up close to the caravan park and saw the perimeter that had been created. There were still paramedics on the scene, and she nipped around the rear of the caravan park, disappearing into the darkness.

One ambulance was close by, and sneaking out from behind the bush, she rounded the front of it before stealing along the side. Then peering into the back, she saw there was no one in there. The paramedics must have been working on somebody out on the field. Kirsten crept inside the truck and heard a voice shouting towards her. She looked around quickly, saw a yellow jacket and a green uniform. Kirsten pulled it on as fast as she could. She was just zipping up the jacket as the voice shouted again and she realised that someone was standing at the edge of the ambulance.

'They're desperate for more help outside.'

'Okay,' said Kirsten. 'I'm on my way.'

She turned around and saw a police constable. 'We're probably going to need more of your guys as well. Several victims fighting for their lives. That's what they were saying.'

'I'm coming,' said Kirsten, reaching up and grabbed a pack from off the shelf. She had no idea what it was, but at least she looked the part as she stepped out of the back of the ambulance and tore off to the scene. As she ran past one victim on the ground, another paramedic shouted at her.

'Come and give us a hand. I need you to hold this for a second.'

Kirsten held down a wound for the man while he wrapped it up, but before he could ask for anything further, she sprinted off. The caravan was a mess, but she needed to know if Johann had gotten away. Kirsten routed over towards it. Taking a glance around to make sure no one was watching her, she took off the yellow jacket and turned it inside out so the black faced out. Kirsten dove underneath the caravan.

She looked up to see if the trapdoor had been activated, but it hadn't and she almost tripped up on a body lying on the ground. Instinctively her hand went down checking the pulse on the neck of the person. It was a small woman. Probably not much bigger than herself, but she was dressed in black. *Infiltration gear* thought Kirsten. *The kind of thing our lot wear.*

There was a weak pulse and she put her hand on the woman's shoulder, pulling it back until the head rolled over to one side. Kirsten almost started. It was Anna Hunt. The woman was a mess, and had clearly been shot.

Kirsten thought quickly about what to do. Anna clearly needed attention. Kirsten stole back out from underneath the caravan, put on the fluorescent jacket with paramedic written and walked directly to the nearest police constable.

'We need more crews. There's a woman under there. Anyone still inside the caravan?'

'We've searched, but no. There's no one in there.'

Blast, thought Kirsten. *They've got him, or somebody's got him. It must be the Russians because Anna Hunt's here.* She knew the site well and there was a CCTV that operated from the cabin at the far end. As she looked across the scene that was lit up by car headlights, she could see that the operations cabin hadn't been opened yet. Everything was still so raw. She turned back to the police constable.

'Call someone in for that one, please? I've got to take an ambulance away.'

'Don't you want to stay with her?'

'You stay, please. I've got to go; it's critical.'

Kirsten ran off as if it really was critical, and sped up to the ambulance she had stolen the clothing from. Peering inside, she saw no one there still. Taking off the yellow jacket and stripping out of the green fatigues, she threw them back inside. Once she got out onto the road, she walked around the edge of the police cordon and continued to where there was no one on the perimeter.

They were obviously assuming everybody would come in via the road, any non-first responders would try and gain access from there. There also wouldn't be enough police constables to form a human ring around the place. Everyone was busy with the wounded, the dying, and the dead. The police wouldn't have a clue what was actually going on, and the services would just react as best they could. You certainly couldn't blame them for that.

Kirsten saw the dark control building, a small brick fixture, and stole through the grass towards it. On arriving, it took her a mere ten seconds to pick the lock and break in. It was the CCTV site for the small caravan park, so it was a wonder sometimes they even locked it.

Once inside, she looked at the system in front of her, and quickly replayed the recorded images. She could see the caravan at the far end of the park, although the camera was not directly aimed at it, and a number of cars had arrived. Then a second set of cars rolled up and a firefight began.

As she watched closely, Kirsten thought she saw Johann being taken inside a car and she stopped the image, zooming in as best she could on the number plate. The car was blue, an old Cavalier by looks of it, with a number plate that ended in YGT. Kirsten quickly tidied up around her, exited the CCTV building and worked her way back towards her car. Once inside, she drove well away from the scene and wondered what she should do.

Anna Hunt was compromised, lying there, possibly dying. The scene had got out of hand. Johann Stein had been taken. Kirsten was wary about calling anyone from the service; after all, she was running rogue from them. Anna had known, that's why she was here in force for Stein. She must have known about the caravan at some point. Or, had Kirsten been traced? Had Kirsten been followed when she dropped him off?

She sat in the car thinking aloud. *I need to get Stein back. I can't go to the agency because if we find him the first thing that will happen is that they'll take him off me. They'll go for what he knows. I need to be able to get him myself. If the agency grabs him, it's game over.*

Kirsten was convinced that the idea of the UK having this

weapon and being able to lord it over every other country was as repugnant as anyone else having it. The best solution was to get rid of it. Again, she thought that might mean getting rid of Stein, but that wasn't something she did.

Kirsten couldn't work through the service, but she still had friends. She could talk to Ross, but it would look bizarre Alan being off work and trying to get access at this time of night. She needed somebody who could operate well, somebody who wouldn't be questioned for what they were doing. Somebody who could access information without looking suspicious.

Justin Chivers was the one, but Kirsten couldn't contact him. After all, he was still working for the service. Anna would be looking for that contact, for Kirsten had worked with Justin before. He'd be an obvious target to be spoken to by her, to be used by her, and so Anna and the service would've put some sort of track around him, monitoring what contacts he had. Then she thought of someone who might just be able to speak to Justin and get a message back to Kirsten without anyone knowing. She spun through the contacts on her phone, saw the name, Dominic, and pressed the call button.

'What the heck,' said the voice on the other end. 'Seriously? Do you know what time it is?'

'Sorry,' said Kirsten. 'Apologies for disturbing you, but I need you.'

'I retired. Do you not get that?' said Dom. 'Remember, we used to work together. Now I'm retired. Carrie-Anne's retired as well. We're not coming back out of retirement.'

'I don't want you out of retirement. I want you to get a message to Justin.'

'A message to Justin? You work with Justin. Remember? We're no longer in the office. You're part of that team.'

'It would appear not.'

There was a silence on the other end of the phone, and Kirsten could hear a whisper. Carrie -Anne must have been lying in the bed beside Dom. The two had disappeared off together at the end of the last mission, decided to go make a life for themselves on the outside. Part of Kirsten was glad they were still together, but she didn't have time to reminisce.

'Dom, listen, I haven't got time. I need Justin to check CCTV around the Riverdale caravan site. There's just been a major incident here and all the roads around it, and you're looking for a Cavalier with registration plate ending YGT. Got it?'

'Got it. Head down, and how does he get back to you?'

'He doesn't. He talks to you. Carrie-Anne rings me.'

'Okay. Do you need anything else?' asked Dom. For a moment, Kirsten found herself ready to say yes. She was ready to say, 'Dom, come and help me; bring Carrie-Anne. Let's work as a team again.' But the pair had left because Dom had had enough of the life. Dom had wanted a chance to go away and to live as a normal person and he wanted to do it with Carrie Ann. If Kirsten brought them back into this, there was a probability they might not walk away. If this went south on Kirsten, she might not just get kicked out of the service, she might get prosecuted; potentially, treason was on the cards.

'No, I'm good,' said Kirsten, 'but I need it fast.'

'Okay,' said Dom, 'I'll close the call.'

Kirsten sat back in the seat, breathed out and tried to relax. Her mind spun to Craig, her lover she'd left at her flat. She reckoned it was brought on by hearing Dom and Carrie-Anne together. At least there was hope. Two people from the service getting out and making a life for themselves. She kicked herself for allowing feelings to interrupt her decision making. It took

143

just over half an hour before the call from Carrie-Anne came back. Kirsten looked at her phone and let it ring for a moment, almost too anxious to pick it up and press the button.

'Yes,' said Kirsten.

'Justin's gone in, tried to get into the system. It's all locked. They're all over it already. If you're going to get onto it, he says, you're going have to contact the service directly. He's not got access to it; they froze him out. What the heck are you into?' asked Carrie-Anne.

'Nothing that need concern you,' she said and hoped that it was coming across with an affectionate tone.

'Well, you need to contact them directly,' said Carrie-Anne. 'If you need us—'

'I won't,' said Kirsten.

'If you need us, and Dom agrees, we've got your back.'

'Thank you, but no,' said Kirsten, rather firmly. 'Thanks for trying. See you around.'

She closed the call. It wasn't fair. She should have had an hour to sit down and chat and talk about old times and see how they were doing, not just pitch in with a call in the middle of the night, but that's what it was. What was more concerning was half an hour of night had gone and she had no further information on where Johann Stein was. She picked up the phone and called a number that she rarely touched.

'Miss Stewart. Well, well, I was wondering when you would call.'

Godfrey sounded different on the phone than when you saw him in person. Kirsten had been brought into the inner circle by him, the head of the service, someone who was very close to Anna Hunt, but Kirsten was also wary, for Godfrey was an experienced handler. He had taught Anna Hunt, and Anna had extreme respect for him on that basis. He could be the most dangerous man.

'Do you know where he is?'

'Why should I tell you?' asked Godfrey.

'Because I'll bring him to you. He'll come to me. I've made contact. You sent Anna in after him, and she's lying in a heap.'

The phone went silent. Kirsten thought she could hear the man breathing heavy.

'Dead?'

'Not when I left her. Paramedics on the scene with her, but it's a right mess up there. This is spiralling out of control, Godfrey. I know what the stakes are, but this needs ending.'

'Agreed,' said Godfrey. 'It does, and it needs ending by you bringing the man to me. I have assets sweeping the area now, although we're shorthanded, thanks to what happened at the caravan site. I was aware there was an incident, but I thought our colleagues had just gone dark.'

'No,' said Kirsten. 'It's a mess.'

'The car was seen approximately twenty minutes north of the caravan park. I've got a small number of detachments fanning out and looking. By all means, go and assist in that number, but your instructions are to bring him in. If you can't, revert to your previous instruction.'

'Of course,' said Kirsten. 'You left me out in the dark. You could have told me what was going on.'

'I know your weakness,' said Godfrey. 'I told it to Anna, but she insisted on taking you onboard and you have so many good qualities. But this . . . this is different.'

'I'll call you when I have him.'

'You make sure you do,' said Godfrey. 'We're not amused at this end.'

Chapter 18

Kirsten drove her car north, realising that the twenty-minutes statement was not a very accurate description. Had it been twenty minutes since the car was spotted on a road cam? Godfrey was giving little away. She was also aware that he had made it quite clear that he was not best amused with what she'd done. Anna Hunt was also lying in a heap. That would grind on him for the two of them were close. Kirsten struggled to call her a friend, and yet the woman had saved her life on the last active mission Kirsten had been on. Still, she hadn't told her what she was doing this time, and if she had been shot, Kirsten was going to be up against some serious opposition.

As she drove along the road, she took out her phone and started scanning the map. There were a number of villages and she would have to take a run through each one. The hour was now four in the morning. It may be another hour or two before sunrise, yet the day was already beginning to permeate through. It was more like a twilight rather than true darkness. Kirsten looked at her watch and realised she was about twenty minutes north of the caravan park and pulled off into the first little village she saw. She drove through but couldn't identify a

Cavalier anywhere, never mind with a YGT on the registration plate.

She drove around the village three times but saw nothing unusual and so continued back to the main road. There was a farmyard further up, and again she drove off up the track but couldn't see anything. As she drove further along, there was a small turning off to a village and the track up to it was single track. As she reached the village, she saw several small houses, almost like a country terrace. There were no lights on in any of them, but she saw cars parked outside. Many of the houses looked like they'd been given a makeover in recent years and a large amount of money probably thrown at them.

Again, there was nothing untoward, no lights on or anybody obvious inside, and as Kirsten spun her car around to leave, it was only as she passed the last house that she thought the car looked out of place. It was old from the number plate, maybe fifteen or sixteen years old. The rest of the cars before the terrace had all been purchased probably within the last five. They were Mercedes or nippy sports cars. This looked like a family run-around, one that had been kicked to pieces over the years.

Kirsten drove her car out of the village and parked it off the road to one side. She had thought about hiding it, but she'd have to drive back to the road and go some distance away and she wanted it close in case she had to get away with Johann Stein. Her man was no athlete after all, and she couldn't drag him forever. Once she had parked the car, Kirsten walked back up the single-track road to the village and stepped off to one side before the houses.

She crept through the long grass that was around her, approaching the older car from the side, and then stopping

147

beside its number plate. She looked at the screws on it. They were recently taken out, and then put back in. It was clear because they were very rusty, but there was no rust around them where they were screwed in.

There was a garage at the end of the terrace and Kirsten walked over to it, keeping her eyes open for anyone around her. She drew her gun, edged up against the garage before opening the door at the side. It wasn't locked, and inside she found a blue Cavalier. Walking to the rear, she checked the number plate and it ended in YGT.

Kirsten slid back out of the garage and knelt down to think about her next plan. The trouble with a terrace was there were only two ways into the house, the front door and the back, and that meant that all the windows were on those sides as well. It wouldn't be easy to go in. She thought she should wait until they brought him out and implement her attack from there, with the element of surprise. If he was inside in a room, she'd have to firefight her way in, and at the end of the day, it was just her and her handgun.

It crossed her mind she could call Dom and Carrie-Anne. They would help provide firepower, but it wasn't an easy scenario, and they hadn't practised for it. The other choice was, of course, to call Godfrey. Then she'd have all the forces at her disposal, but they'd also take Stein. Trying to grab him right from under their noses would not be easy.

Daylight was approaching and Kirsten did not like the position she was sitting in. The approach from the front would be dodgy and her car was also sitting by the single road. So, she stole back, retrieved her car, and drove it back to the main road where she parked it up in a small layby sheltered from the main road by trees.

Kirsten reached into her car but instead of her black jacket, she now put on a green camouflaged one with a green hat on her head and put on some green camouflage leggings. When there were no cars around, she crossed the road, walked up the side of the road towards the small village before plonking herself down in the grass. She wouldn't move, but simply lie there and watch what was going on.

Beside her, she had brought several devices that she could throw across the road, capable of shredding a car's tires in an instant. If they tried to drive him away, she'd stop them, take them out, and then run for her car. It wasn't the best of plans, but at least it meant they couldn't simply just drive off. From inside her jacket, she drew out a small pair of binoculars, incredibly powerful for the size of them, and began watching the house.

It was in the middle of the morning that Kirsten received a text on her phone. It was from Carrie-Anne with one word saying, 'Assistance?' Kirsten realised that this could be what she needed: friends, people to help break in with her, get Stein, but then they were implicated as well. She couldn't do that to them. Dom had wanted out, but he had stayed for Carrie-Anne until she was ready to go. Besides, after what happened last time, Kirsten didn't even know how they would be, mentally. She nearly lost them.

As Kirsten was lying in the grass, she suddenly thought she could see movement further out in the fields. She pulled the binoculars to her eyes. *No, there wasn't, was there? There wasn't anything there or was there?*

She crawled forward, keeping down on her belly until she could get closer to the house. She scanned the surroundings with her binoculars and thought she saw movement off to

149

the left. She suddenly identified a head, though it was brief and disappeared back down quickly. But it was a mistake. Cautiously, she edged back to her previous position, so she was located beside the tire-shredding devices that she'd brought along.

She dialled a number on her phone. She had an idea of who was out there, but she needed to confirm it; after all, she didn't want to go shooting her own people.

'Stewart, I take it you have him for me then.'

'You know I know where he is. What did you do?'

'Your car was on satellite. We followed you. What did you see? Why is he in there?'

'Old car, one old car amongst a lot. They weren't stupid enough to leave the Cavalier right in the open, but they were stupid enough to leave something that didn't look like it belonged. Cavalier's in the garage, beside the house. Are you watching this?'

'I have a feed.'

'I wouldn't go for him. Not now, I'd wait for him coming out,' said Kirsten.

'I'm afraid not,' said Godfrey. 'The longer we wait, the more likely other people will find them as well.'

'Others,' said Kirsten, slightly surprised. 'The Russians have him. You're here for him. Who are the others?'

'Dear girl, you didn't really think there were just two sides involved here? Everyone's out. I've been feeding false information to our American colleagues to keep them off our backs. They're currently looking for him somewhere in Glasgow. Not doing a good job of it either. Of course, the Israelis are there too. Thankfully, they haven't shot at each other yet though. Been selling stories to everyone. Planting false leads.'

'Why did you send me after him,' asked Kirsten. 'If you knew I'd keep him away from you, why did you send me after him?'

'Because we couldn't find him,' said Godfrey, 'and Anna said you would, and she was right. We were missing something in his background, and you found him. Where was he?'

'Oban,' said Kirsten. 'What you didn't do was find out about his resources; he was using them. He had a holiday home he let out. Georgina Rogers booked it two weeks every year. She's actually his lover. They met a number of years ago and then they get back every year because they can't leave it alone. He reached out to her for help.'

'What did you do at our storage facility?'

'I made sure that the Russians couldn't get something that could lead to something quite devastating. The ingredients were there.'

'That's where he put them,' said Godfrey. 'Not to mind though; once we have him, we'll be able to reproduce.'

'Why? Why reproduce?'

'Because it keeps us on top. We can't have the country being threatened and it will give us certain leverage.'

'Not if you never use it.'

'Oh, they know we'll use it. I mean the UK has a history of using things in the past. More recently, we haven't had to.'

'More recently, we haven't always had the upper hand.'

'Don't be a fool, Miss Stewart. Every nation would use it if they have it. Every nation will threaten with it.'

'Then better for every nation not to have it. For it not to be there.'

'If you felt like that, you should have shot him, killed him where he stood. He has what we need. There are no records of it. We have scanned through everything. We have gone over and over our facilities. Johann Stein has cleaned everything out and now you've assisted him. Be careful you're not standing on the wrong side here. Be very careful.'

Kirsten glanced through her binoculars and could see figures beginning to move towards the house.

'This is not the way to do it, Godfrey. Not the way. It won't get you what you want, either.'

'Oh, it will,' said Godfrey. 'They won't kill him. They'll hang on to the last. We'll go in with plenty of force; they won't know what hit them. Then we'll squirrel him away until he tells us what we need to know, and then, well, then, we'll make sure nobody else can get the information because that's what you can't do. That's your flaw. The trouble with having a moralistic centre is it can never outweigh what needs to be done, Ms Stewart. What needs to be done now is that information should be extracted from Mr Stein and then Mr Stein should be placed in a situation where he cannot divulge it ever again. The only situation that I've ever known to be one hundred percent effective is, sadly, if the man is dead. I suggest you stay out of this one. Don't run in like a hero. Let the team go in and bring Mr Stein to me. I still have a use for you. You can still be part of the team. You did call in for Anna.'

Kirsten could feel the adrenaline pumping within her veins, fuelled by anger. *You don't just play with somebody's life like this*, she thought. *You just don't treat a man like he's nothing but a piece of information.* When she was working as a detective, it was all about the person, understanding those you caught even and still having respect for them. You cared for their situation, but Godfrey was cold, clinical, and he said that she had a flaw!

It wasn't a flaw. It was never a flaw. Kirsten reached down

for the spikes that lay beside her. On her knees, she crawled over to the road and threw the spikes across them. Looking up, she saw the charge on the house begin, several forces moving towards it. She stood up out of the grass, a gun in her hand. 'I won't go down without fighting for him. Nobody should have this,' she said and replied to herself, 'Nobody.'

With that, she took off over the grass, running up the side of the road, watching the service, those who previously she'd have thought of colleagues even though she didn't know them. She stared as they broke into the house, kicking through the front door, and gunfire rang throughout the area.

Stein, she thought, *go get Stein*.

Chapter 19

The gunfire from the house echoed around the surrounding landscape. Kirsten ran as hard as she could, her handgun held in front of her, waiting for anyone to try to stop her. Her one goal was to get Johann Stein out of the building and away to safety, but she knew it would be a tall order, as there were too many people involved now and everywhere she looked, she saw somebody attacking the house.

From inside, there were cries and shouts. Kirsten saw the front door exploding open, gunfire coming from inside and one of the service operators being shot in the stomach and thrown backwards. They had gone in with such force, windows breaking, smoke grenades thrown inside, but the initial shove had been pushed back, leaving the service holding a perimeter of approximately ten metres lying low on the grass.

This was not good. Kirsten reckoned she would have a better chance if the service had got inside. She could have followed up behind them. Part of her was wondering how the service would react to her. Had they been told to shoot her? At the end of the day, Johann Stein was the main objective. If they didn't come away with Stein, they were coming away with nothing.

After what Godfrey would've seen as a betrayal, as opposed to a mild wobbling, Kirsten wouldn't have been surprised if someone had been ordered to put a bullet in her.

Rather than approach from the rear, Kirsten ran up beside the house, hearing a couple of shots skim off the ground beside her. She dove into the garage, knowing the blue Cavalier would be in there and climbed inside, clocking the key still in ignition. After firing it up, she reversed, breaking open the garage doors, racing backwards across the street. There was no curb on the other side, merely a grass area, and she had to spin the car around to keep it on the tarmac section.

Once she'd driven back a considerable distance, she took the car out of reverse, put down the accelerator and drove at the large bay window of the house. The car mounted the small curb that ran in front of the terrace, and Kirsten opened the car door, throwing herself out. The car was hurtling now and crashed hard into the brick wall of the house causing the window above to shatter.

She rolled away. The bonnet of the car went on fire, and Kirsten could hear shouts from inside. There was a small tree across from where the car had crashed, and Kirsten rolled in behind it, putting her back up against it, hoping it would provide her with enough protection from any shots from the house. She looked to her right and saw one of the service operators taking out some more smoke grenades and throwing them towards the bay window. From her left she heard a shout, a woman standing in her dressing gown, dog at her feet. The dog began to bark and take off with all the noise and Kirsten saw her begin to run out after it.

'Get back, get the hell back in the house,' shouted Kirsten to the woman, but she paid her no heed, instead racing after her little dog. Kirsten rolled out from behind the tree, ran over and knocked the woman flat on the ground.

'What the hell are you doing? Get back in the house. There's a bloody gunfight going on out here.'

'Jake, get Jake,' said the woman. The dog was running around in rings yelping, clearly panicked by all that was going on.

'You go inside,' said Kirsten. 'I'll get him.'

She watched the woman pick herself up and run for her house. If there was one thing Kirsten was sure of, if Jake wasn't coming back towards her, she was not running around here in the open trying to get him. She watched as the dog veered this way and that across the road. Then it turned and ran back, at first heading towards the house and then cutting back towards the tree. Kirsten rolled over, reached out with both hands and grabbed the animal as it raced past. It fought with its paws, and she could feel the claws scraping into her arms, but she was able to drive herself up from her knees and run back to the woman's house, throwing the dog inside.

'Just stay in,' said Kirsten, and stood at the door, looking out.

'Thank you,' said the woman. 'My Jake.'

Kirsten could hear the tears. 'If you've got a basement,' said Kirsten, 'get in it and stay there.'

'We haven't got one. I'll hide upstairs.'

She saw the service personnel who'd thrown the smoke grenades at the bay window begin to race forward and split to either side of the car that had crashed into the front of the building. On seeing this, she ran out, sweeping around behind them and realised that they were going either side of the car to then go in. The car was on fire, and with the smoke, it was generating, along with that from the grenades that had been thrown in, she couldn't see anything inside, but there were shots being fired.

She ran directly up behind the car, jumped up onto the boot, scrambled over the top of the roof and was about to run in through the flames when she saw the two personnel beside her fall backwards hitting the ground. Kirsten took her gun and fired widely giving a deadly sweep throughout the smoke-filled room. She felt the flames briefly lick her as she put a foot on the hot bonnet before diving into the room.

Kirsten had no idea where she was arriving, and she thought she landed at first on some sort of a coffee table before falling off it. Smoke grenades had made the place thick with a dense screen that had a cloy taste to it.

Kirsten rolled and hit the edge of what she thought was a sofa and scrambled round it. As she was going down to the small side of it, her hand touched somebody's forehead. There was a quick panic from the person, and Kirsten too, as they grappled in the dark. There could have been a gun there, Kirsten didn't know, but she found the person's throat and her arms sunk around him.

Over the top of her, bullets were firing here and there, and she was turned as he lifted her head up. Whoever it was, he was strong and managed to turn Kirsten onto her back, hands were placed on her throat, and she thought that the person was extending them, pushing down on her throat, but that, in turn, raised the perpetrator up. At some point, a bullet must have hit him for the arms collapsed. They pitched forward and Kirsten ended up throwing him off her.

If there's no basement, she thought, *they must have him upstairs. I'm going to need to go up and get him.* Slowly, she crawled around the rear of the sofa and found herself touching a rear wall. She traced along it to find another wall and then the edge of the door. Kirsten stayed on her knees, struggling to see more than about two feet in front of her, but she negotiated around the open door that led out into the hallway beyond. As she looked up, she saw feet stepping down the stairs, and suddenly someone was shouting out of the window.

'We have Stein,' he yelled. 'Stop or we'll kill him.'

Kirsten wondered what the response would be. Stein's death wouldn't be a disaster, at least not in her eyes, for the man's secret would die with him. It depended on how badly Godfrey wanted this secret, how badly her own country did. She could hear some murmuring from outside and then a loud 'Cease fire!' coming from one of the officers. Kirsten retreated into the room as a number of feet came down the stairs. She saw a pair of hands tied behind a back. *That must be Stein*, she thought. As he was brought down to the front door, the man who had shouted earlier asking for a ceasefire spoke again.

'I wish to meet to discuss terms. Neither of us are going to win from this position. We need to talk.'

Kirsten wondered what agreement they could come to. After all, her own service wanted the man, the Russians wanted the man, and neither wanted the other side to have him. What was the compromise? A bullet in the man's head so nobody got him? She didn't understand the tactic, except that it probably could provide some rest and respite in the middle of what was a ferocious battle. But as she looked up at the man with the hands tied behind his back, she realised it wasn't Stein. He was around the same height, but it wasn't him.

Behind the man were four other people of whom three held guns. They were all were masked up, but one wasn't holding a weapon. *Why not?* she thought. Then it dawned on her—*that's Stein. They're actually going to sneak him out*. Kirsten held her ground within the room as she heard the man disappear out of the front door to go and negotiate. Inside there was little talk, and slowly the smoke began to clear from within the room; the car fire was now smouldering.

When the man came back inside the house, she heard him speaking Russian and the little she could make out mentioned something about retreat. The man pretending to be Stein was left with this colleague in the middle of the hallway while the four other men stepped away.

Maybe that was it. He had actually said he was going to exchange Stein for their safety. Had someone on the other side fallen for that? Kirsten watched the party of four, all masked up, step into the kitchen and start to make for the door. The original speaker and the man pretending to be Stein moved to the front door. Kirsten snuck out, following the others through into the kitchen and watched them disappear out to the rear of the house.

She watched them walk out, turn right behind the house and she peered up over through the window. She could see the service personnel watching them. *Surely somebody would clock this*, she thought. *Won't they? They'll be under orders not to fire.*

Kirsten followed the men out of the rear door around the side of the house. They didn't see her, but she knew the service personnel could see her. She held one hand up to them indicating that they shouldn't fire. It was certainly a risk, for maybe they would protect what ground they had made. But, on the other hand, any gunshots now could end this cease fire that they had. If someone had agreed to it, they must have believed that they would get what they wanted in the end.

Kirsten wondered how she should play this. She was there behind her target, and she knew who Stein was. He didn't have a weapon. How had somebody from the service not caught on that he didn't have a weapon? She stole up behind them, knowing there was only one route here. Because there were three of them, she would have to incapacitate them all; more than that, she'd then have to get on the run with Stein to do that. She'd need to get inside one of the other houses. From there, she could come out the front, take a car and make off.

Kirsten steeled herself. Stein was a person, a decent person in this case, trying to prevent thousands if not millions from dying, keen to prevent any country from taking on and wiping out the other. All he wanted was his freedom afterwards. He deserved that, but it meant that Kirsten was going to have to do something she didn't like. These three men wouldn't see her coming, but there was no choice. Was there?

She stole up behind them. The first one she struck with an incredibly hard blow across the back of the head with her gun, and the man tumbled forward. By the time the other two had turned to face her, she was firing shots at them and they dropped. She grabbed the mask of the person without the gun and lifted it seeing Stein's shocked face. She reached up, grabbing him by the collar, operating in the few seconds of shock and confusion she had created and drove him hard across the driveway of the next door's house. She hit the back door with her shoulder, and while it bounced, it remained firm. Her hand dropped down to the handle.

They had actually left the back door open in the middle of all this. She threw Stein inside, closing the door and hearing shots peppering from outside. What sort of reaction did she expect from the service? They had suddenly seen Stein being taken away by someone else, by a third party. She wasn't Russian, but neither was she service anymore or so it seemed. Kirsten pushed him through the house and saw the woman whose dog she'd rescued, looking amazed at her.

'Car keys,' said Kirsten. 'Where's your car keys.' The woman reached forward onto her table and threw them up to her. Kirsten grabbed Stein and kept Stein moving through the house, holding him by the back of the neck.

'When we get out here, you go into the car. They'll not shoot at you. They'll only shoot at me if they get a clear shot.'

'Where do we go from there?' asked Stein.

'Don't you worry. That's my job.' They reached the front door and Kirsten told Stein to open it. As he did so, Kirsten could see the guns trained at her and put Stein out in front of her, making sure any shot towards her had the risk of taking him out. She had to be careful. Maybe the Russians would shoot as well, now they'd seemingly lost.

'Open the passenger door. I get in first and you follow me in, okay?' Kirsten backed into the car and saw the button to start it. It was one of those newer cars and the key simply in your pocket was enough to make the systems come on. She had to slide over into the seat, however, her gun still on Stein's head. But once she dropped the clutch, the car started.

She didn't wait, put it into reverse, and drove out erratically, hitting a car behind her. She spun the wheel and drove past, her head simply down, telling Stein to do the same. She guessed roughly where the heat from the roadside would come from.

As the glass of the front window of the car blew out, she rounded the corner. She glanced briefly up to see the long straight road ahead of her out to the main junction, but she also saw where she had laid the spikes to disable any car following her. As the car reached them, the tires blew out. She skidded, but she pulled on the handbrake and managed to leave the car lying across the road.

From inside her jacket, she took out a grenade, pulled the pin and threw it into the back. 'Go,' she shouted at Stein, telling him to get out of the car. She cleared from the driver's side and ran off into the field closely followed by him. Once she thought she was clear enough, she waited for him and then threw him to the ground as the car exploded. There was probably shock back up the road, but Kirsten knew they weren't getting any cars out quickly. She also knew where hers was on a lay-by. She grabbed Stein by the collar. 'We go again, come on.' She now had a gap. All she had to do was maintain it.

Chapter 20

As they ran through the layby, past the large trees that sheltered the car from the road, Kirsten saw Stein's face. The man was exhausted, terrified, and she had to open the car door for him and throw him into the passenger seat. She jumped into the driver's side, put her foot to the floor and drove off, looking up and down the road quickly to see if anyone was about. They could be tracking her from the air as well, so she needed to get away quickly.

'We need to get you to ground,' said Kirsten driving along. 'Get you off the grid. I can find you somewhere, but following that, we need you out of the country. You can't be on the run here. Too many places, too many faces, too many people can see you. There are cameras everywhere. They will find you.'

'I know,' he said. 'I know. I guess they're already all over here looking for us.'

'You better believe it,' said Kirsten, 'but I've got an idea. It'll be about another two or three minutes.' The car fell into silence as Kirsten continued up the road north before she saw some large green sheds.

'What's that?' asked Stein.

'That is Scottish gold. That's where they keep the whisky.

Well, that's where they mature it. Stored inside the casks to get the flavour. Sits there for a long time and it's heavily secured, but I can get us in. The good side is there's not that many people hanging around it. If they've seen my car, I can park this elsewhere. I'll store you first and then I'll come back.'

'We can't stay there for long, can we? We're going to need food.'

'Food you'll have. I'll bring some back.'

Kirsten turned off the road onto the side road that led up the side of the large green sheds. She could see the cameras pointing up and down the outside, but after having parked the car off in a wooded area, she stole back with Stein, making sure that she watched the sweep of the camera as it moved up and down the side of the building. She avoided it neatly before breaking in through the door. Once inside, she led Stein round the rear of several large barrels, and gave him a gun.

'You don't use that unless you have to,' said Kirsten. 'Trust me, it's not a good idea to fire it unless you intend to kill.'

Stein looked at her. 'Then don't give me it. I won't kill with it. That's the whole point, isn't it?' he said. 'I don't want people to be decimated. I don't want nations destroyed. What I found out, what I saw being built, what I conceived, it was horrific in the moment of excitement, I suddenly saw what I'd become and done. I won't kill anyone,' he said, handing back the gun.

'Okay,' said Kirsten, 'stay here. I'll be back shortly.'

She snuck back out, avoiding the cameras again, this time driving to a nearby housing estate. She watched closely to see whether there was a house with no one in that she could infiltrate. Having identified one, she took the car back out and parked it a little distance away. Kirsten then proceeded back to the house, jumped over the rear fence, and broke in through the door to the kitchen. Once inside, she lifted food from the fridge, anything that didn't have to be cooked, as well as a number of drinks. By the time the owner would discover that they'd been raided, Kirsten had returned to Stein.

She found the man asleep but then again, he must have been exhausted because she was. And she was used to being shot at, not that it ever became any more pleasant. Kirsten let the man sleep. Settling down, she broke up some cheese and added a can of fizzy blackcurrant. It wasn't the most splendid meal she'd ever had, but she was starving. She then took some of the sliced meat, left enough for Stein and allowed herself to drift off into her sentry mode. Her eyes closed; her senses stayed alert. She remained like this until she heard Stein waking up.

'There's plenty of food there if you want it,' said Kirsten. She needn't have said it twice because the man was ravenous. Once he'd finished, Kirsten saw him becoming nervous again.

'I don't get how this is going to work,' said Kirsten. 'Where are you going to go? Where in this world can you go that you'll be safe?'

'You get me out of here,' said Stein. 'Just get me out of here.'

'No,' said Kirsten. 'I need to know where you intend to go.'

'If you get me on a plane out of here, get me to South America. From there, I'll find one of the ships that works down close to Antarctica, a ship where I can hide away as the cleaner or something. I'll get myself a new name and once there I'm just going to work, keep a low profile.'

'Then what?' asked Kirsten.

'Well, my work, they'll be able to find an antidote for it. That was one of the things. I cracked how to deliver it, this virus. They always said that the work for the antidote would be five to ten years away. In five to ten years' time, my weapon's obsolete. As soon as they've got that antidote, it's gone. Then I can come back out.'

'You truly believe that? Some of these people in this business, they're very vindictive. They settle those scores.'

'It's just a risk I'll have to take,' he said, 'but it's one worth taking. I still want a life at the end of this. Just because I'm doing the right thing doesn't make me a martyr. I'm not looking to be one.'

Kirsten stared at the man as he picked up another piece of cheese, placing it in his mouth and chewing it slowly. How was she meant to shoot him when his moral standards compared to Godfrey or Anna Hunt were catastrophically higher?

And that was the problem with him. Everyone else she killed in this line of work was because they were doing something against her. They were preventing her from doing her job or they were actively going after someone else. Kill or be killed. Even those three she'd had to take out rescuing Stein. She was rescuing him; she could justify it. She couldn't justify this man's death, just because others were seeking him. He'd done the right thing. He was destroying all knowledge of his new weapon because he realised how dangerous it was. Didn't that deserve some sort of reward?

Kirsten could smell the wood all around her and began to realise how it infected the whisky. Infected was a strange choice of words because that meant that the whisky wasn't some sort of beautiful creation but rather something that has been taken hold of, moulded to a certain way. That's how she felt with the service.

Once she'd been on a train, stopping it from blowing a hole out of London. She felt then she was in something that she could be proud of, something that was her, but this was totally different. How could you justify to yourself killing a man like this, upright, upstanding, sacrificial? Better than most of the rest she'd seen. She also wasn't happy she had been messed about.

If I had a defect, she thought, *why did they take me on? Why did they keep pushing? Oh, it's okay. We'll use Kirsten because she's good at this bit. She can get that bit done. Oh, by the way, we'll just destroy any moral compass you have. I was a detective constable. I was there bringing people to justice; I was there assisting some of the best to stop some of the most heinous crimes. What have I become? They're trying to make me an assassin, and not even a long-distance one, one that gets up in the face, finds out if you're going to do what we say, and if not, just blows you away.'*

She felt a hand touch her on the arm and looked over at Johann Stein.

'Are you okay?' he asked. 'I think you're finding this hard.'

'It's okay,' she said, 'it's just what I do.'

'No,' he said. 'They want you to kill me. If I don't come with them, they want me dead. They sent you to come and get me. You found me where nobody else did, but you're not happy about it. You haven't taken me in to discuss it with them, so you don't trust them. You don't trust them to have this weapon and not use it, do you?'

'No,' said Kirsten, 'I don't. I'm not trusting very many people at the moment including yourself. Everything you say is okay. It sounds laudable, but ultimately, I don't know you from anyone else. You could be playing me just to get away to where you want to go. Maybe you've got some interest in a small faction, a tiny country. I don't know and I see great sense in dispatching you,' said Kirsten. 'It's just not fair, though, because at the moment, I can't see you've done anything wrong.'

167

'You've walked into something, and you don't like where it's got you,' he said. 'You're like me in that.' His hand picked up another piece of cheese, which he threw from one hand to the other rather than eat. 'We're both like this cheese. Here it is, its purpose to be eaten, and this man is just throwing it from side to side, not allowing it to do its purpose. Your purpose is to find out the things that are wrong and put them right. You're not a loudmouth assassin; you can't be. My job is to explore the secret, the boundaries and break them, but they threw me a bite and made me into a killer, someone who can kill millions in a matter of days, all for their own agenda, all for their own money. That's what it's all about. Money here, money there, power.

'We can say we're going to do this and then that country has to give us this A, B, and C. What can they do about it? Nothing. Because it's going to take them five to ten years to even think of an antidote. What does the power that created it do? Oh, hang on to it. They don't turn around and say, 'We should bury this. This is just not worth it.' No, they keep going, and that's the problem. There is no global community, there is only us and what we want, our little faction, be that the UK, be that Russia, be that America, Israel, or whoever.

'One day I have to believe that the world can actually exist coherently. It can look out for each other as countries. We always say we can do it as people, but as soon as we gather around our own particular agendas, it all falls apart. I should be allowed to put this back in its box, but they don't let me. Maybe I was naive enough to think that whatever I came up with, in terms of my inventions, or in terms of my research, would be mine. It's never been mine; it's always been theirs, because it's always been following their agenda.

'Why is the money there? The money is there because it wants to either make more money or control the money that's already out there.'

The man's head went forward into his hands, and he began to cry. Kirsten gave him the dignity of not looking at him, and instead stood up and walked around to the far end of the massive barrel they were behind. She looked at the date on it. There was still a large number of years of maturing for this whisky to be done.

'You can't make a whisky in a day, Stein,' she said to him, 'and you can't change the world either. It's like this whisky, isn't it? It has to infuse the flavour, has to come out of these barrels and into the liquid, but it has to do it slowly. You can't drive it in. It'll be the same with the world. One day it will get there, but it will take time and it will be slow.'

Stein looked up and laughed. 'How can you say that looking at who you work for? There's no good nature here, it's all just greed, and death to those who get in their way. I need to go and hide because the least you're thinking is it will take a long time before it even becomes vaguely possible for me to be free. When they find a cure, it will be my freedom, not until then. The only other way to free me is to die, and I'm not going to play their game for that.'

Kirsten nodded and advised the man he should get some more sleep, but she was troubled. What was she to do with him? Would she be able to keep things going? Get him out? As she stood looking at the stamp on the side of a large whisky barrel, the face that kept coming to her was that of Craig. What do they think of him now? If indeed he was hers, and not theirs? She knew, though, didn't she? From that touch, from the way he had saved her before.

She sat down trying her best to start looking at the positives. There didn't seem to be that many.

Chapter 21

The hour was three in the morning, and Kirsten couldn't sleep. Still holed up behind a whisky barrel in the storage compound, she felt her back beginning to ache, for she was sleeping upright. She felt quite safe, for it was unlikely that anyone would think of checking these large warehouses. Johann and she had eaten earlier on that night, and they were in no danger of running out of food or water, at least for the next twenty-four hours. The difficulty was the next move.

The Russians were seeking Johann. The service was seeking Johann. Various other countries had no doubt heard about the shootout at the house not that far away, and were seeking Johann. He was the man everybody wanted, and yet a man who didn't want to go to any of them. A man who feared that being found by any of them would lead to irreparable damage on the world scene.

Kirsten didn't understand any of the technology, not on any deep level, but she did trust him that what was in his head was toxic to the world. She thought about the fact that the idea of security was dependent upon everybody else having just about the same abilities. *The idea that it's better for me to be working with you than actually being able to take over as the losses I might suffer may be too great.* She thought it was a horrible worldview, even though it may be an accurate one. Kirsten stood up and stretched, and saw Johann open an eye.

'I'm just going out for a bit,' she said. 'I may be gone a number of hours. Don't move. If I'm not back in twenty-four, think about what you do next because you'll be on your own.'

'Where are you going?' asked Johann quietly.

'I'm going for advice.'

'To get us out of here? To look for a route?'

'Yes, absolutely.'

Inside, Kirsten thought that was never the idea. She wanted to check on her moral compass, wanted to know where she was sitting at the moment. Kirsten had, in effect, betrayed the service, but she thought the service was out of line. The UK was out of line. Everyone was out of line at the moment. If she was wrong, she could be throwing away her life, not just her career.

As she worked out of the whisky compound, past the cameras out into the fields, Kirsten wondered what the best way was to get hold of a moral check. She needed to get hold of him, the best moral compass she'd ever known. Then she had an idea.

Kirsten walked until she found a small village, broke into a car, managed to start it, and drove for Inverness. On arrival at the city, she made for the police station where she parked at the rear. In the car was a large rain jacket which she put on and covered her face with the hood, before marching up to the rear doors as if it was the most normal thing in the world. As she entered, a constable came over to her, and she stopped before looking up into his face.

'Excuse me,' she said, 'I've got information for Macleod.'

'The inspector's not here, he'll be at home. Can I take you to somebody else?'

'No, I need to speak to Macleod, and I need to go up to his office to do it.'

'I'm afraid we don't just wander around the police station, ma'am. I can take you down to . . . ' The man looked down and there was a gun pointing at his belly.

'Let's go to Macleod's office,' she said.

This could have gone one of two ways. Either the team were in, in which case she'd say hello to Ross, the new woman Urquhart, or even to Hope McGrath and they could call Macleod for her, or there might not be anybody there, and she was going to have to get this constable to do it.

On arriving at the correct floor, the constable tried to make a turn towards the wrong office and Kirsten corrected him, advising him not to be so stupid in the future. The office was dark when they entered, and Kirsten told the man to walk right through to Macleod's personal office and to sit down in his chair. Kirsten then edged to the desk, still pointing the gun at the man, and told him to phone Macleod. He rang Macleod's number and advised the inspector that he was required immediately, due to a case. Kirsten had provided the words, and because the voice was coming from someone that worked at the station, anyone tapping the phone line wouldn't bat an eyelid. Kirsten then sat down on the floor, gun still pointed at the constable who was sitting, shaking on Macleod's chair. There would probably be a half-an-hour wait. Macleod was never tardy in his arrivals.

It was a half an hour later when Macleod strolled through his office door, flicked on the lights, and stared at the man occupying his seat.

'What are you doing?' asked Macleod. When the man's eyes turned to the floor, Kirsten stood up.

'Sorry to approach you in this way, Seoras, but I had to. Anybody could have been listening to me.'

Macleod took off his coat and hung it up. 'What do you need from me?' he asked directly, almost dispassionately.

'We need this constable to go somewhere where he's not going to hear anything, but he's not going to go and tell anybody, either.'

Macleod walked over to the desk, put two hands down on it and stared at the man. 'Adams, isn't it?' he said.

'Yes, Inspector, Constable Adams. Just covering the back door tonight.'

'I had wondered why no one even looked over at me on the way in. You're going to go back down to that door, Constable Adams. When anybody comes in, you're going to check them in as normal. You're going to look at them and you are going to smile. You're not going to give any reference to what's going on up here. Do you understand me?'

'Yes, sir,' said the man. 'But she was holding a gun at me.'

'That's because she couldn't have got here without holding a gun to you. Don't worry; she's on our side.'

Kirsten was just simply thankful that the man came from a time after Kirsten was at the station, so he didn't know her face.

'You'll also forget you ever saw her. I won't ask you to lie. If someone asks you a direct question, you can, of course, tell them, but you will not mention in conversation or in passing to anyone that you've just been brought up here at gunpoint and asked to phone me. Do I make myself clear?'

'Evidently, sir.'

'Good,' said Macleod. 'It's a matter of national security. Now, back to your job, Constable, and thank you.' The man walked out of the room and Macleod looked over at Kirsten. 'What can I do? Clearly, something's up.'

'First thing for you today is to sit down in that chair of yours or go and get a coffee. Then if anyone comes in, you can pretend you're working.'

'It's four in the morning,' said Macleod. 'I'm in here working on my own without the team. That looks mighty suspicious, but you're in luck because Hope and Clarissa Urquhart will be coming any moment. Well, actually I said I'd take a look at it first. It'll be about half an hour.'

'Well, I better make this quick,' said Kirsten, and sat back down on the floor, her back up against the wall, looking at Macleod. 'There's a situation come up.'

'No details,' said Macleod. 'I don't want any details.'

'I won't give you any,' said Kirsten. 'It will put you in jeopardy, so let's say things hypothetically. We've got a person, or may have, who has something everybody wants. Something that would give everyone the upper hand. So much so, they could dictate terms on everything, and possibly for the next twenty years. That person built something or created something of which we have destroyed the physical specimen, but in their head, there still resides the knowledge and the know-how to reproduce. They don't want to; they want to hide away until such times as something will be made to counter these things, but that relies on them not getting caught. We, however, want to bring him in and hold onto it, saying that we'll never use it, which I distinctly think is a lie. The opportunity for dominating other parties is too great. The person wants to get out. I currently have them away from everyone, and I can either let them get out or I can complete my task, which is to bring them in, or if they don't want to come, kill them.'

Macleod had been sitting looking intent, but now he stood up, began to shake his head, and walked over to the window. It was dark outside, so he clearly wasn't having a peek at the view, even if there was the odd light scattered about. 'Go on,' he said.

'It'll be tough, but I might be able to get them away, then it would be up to them to stay out of the way. I'm not sure that will happen, so I'm left in a quandary. I think the right thing to do is to get them away, to give them that opportunity. I don't want to bring them in because I don't trust the people I'm working for. On the other hand, the obvious solution that would stop said items being a threat would be simply to eliminate this person. I don't think that's right either. It's not that I'm afraid to kill; I have killed plenty.' Macleod looked over briefly, concern on this face. 'It's more to do with the fact that this wouldn't be in self-defence or even in the protection of anything. It would just be cold murder.'

Macleod turned back to the desk, and he put up a hand to Kirsten before walking out into the office. She watched him as he made coffee, knowing he'd be churning over what she had said in his head. Five minutes later, he brought in two steaming cups.

'Firstly, that's a bad idea,' said Kirsten. 'Because if anybody comes in now, you've put two cups of coffee for one person, and having known you from previous, you don't sit there with lots of coffee cups. You would take it back and you'd charge it up again, and secondly, you've just wasted five minutes.'

'Let's get this straight,' said Macleod. 'You need a cup of

coffee; I'm giving you one. If anybody comes in here and questions me over a coffee cup, I will run them out of this office, and besides, there's nothing wrong with having one waiting for Hope or Clarissa, and if they're first then, it won't matter much because they'll cover for you.' He handed over the cup of coffee and Kirsten took it gratefully, sipping the hot liquid.

'On the other point, are you looking for direction or validation?'

'Probably validation,' said Kirsten.

'So, you know what to do. Your mind's made up.'

'Yes. I want to get them away. It's risky. Could die in the effort. Could end up leaving them in the hands of a side even worse than our own.'

'So why are you here?' asked Macleod. 'You don't need me to validate your thoughts. You work in that world, not me. You've chosen not to follow your orders because you think the issue outweighs what you've been told to do. You think there's a better solution. I'm a detective inspector on a murder team. I find out what happened. I don't predict the future.'

'No, but you do have a good head on your shoulders. You do understand the issues.'

'So do you. You don't need me to validate; you know what my answer is. The real question you're asking is, how can I stay in this operation? How can I still be an operative? Why am I an operative when they hand me these things to do?'

'That's right. You're absolutely right, Seoras.'

'As I see it, they wanted you for lots of skills and abilities, and you have them in abundance. I was sorry when you left the team, but you would've been stifled here by us working under Hope and me. You could outshine the pair of us at times. One thing I will say, when they took you on board, they did ask me whether you're unscrupulous or not, whether you could be trusted, and I told them. I told them, "If you break her moral boundary, she'll react the other way." That I thought that was one of the best qualities you had, and I thought maybe you could do something for that service. Maybe it doesn't work that way. I don't know; I've never been there.'

Kirsten drank the rest of her coffee and then stood up, leaving the empty cup on Macleod's desk.

'I'm sorry to have dragged you out.'

'I'm not,' said Macleod. 'I'm always here. The team acts like I'm some person who shouldn't be touched, inconvenienced. When I was the boss, you could always have come to me. You're now my friend; you get even bigger privileges that way.' Kirsten walked forward and put her arms around Macleod, and the two of them hugged for a brief moment.

'I'll miss the lot of you,' said Kirsten.

'I'm going to miss you. Be wise. I may not see you for a long time with what you're doing and what I think it is, so take good care of yourself.'

'Will do, Seoras. Love to the team. Of course, you can't tell them I was here.'

Kirsten turned, put on the jacket which she had found in the car, and as she was opening the door, Macleod called after her.

'Can you tell Ross I'll see him after he's done then? Knew something was up. Ross would never have that long off work. Even when they shot him, he struggled to stay off.'

Kirsten turned back and smiled. 'Thank you, Seoras. I'll see you again.'

'Make sure you do,' Macleod said, his face full of concern. Kirsten just smiled and left the building.

Chapter 22

Given the hour of the morning, Kirsten was able to return the car before the owner had even got out of bed. Although it was daylight by the time she got back inside the whisky barrel compound, she was able to do so with ease as there was no one around. Johann seemed delighted to see her, but she simply nodded at him and indicated she was going to get some sleep. She lay down and went into that sentry sleep, the one where she was on the edge of being awake, ready for any noise, any sign that shouldn't be there.

Kirsten managed to half sleep for about six hours before she woke up, had a drink of water and a few more bites of the cheese that she had brought the previous night. Her conversation with Macleod was still running through her head, but she'd come to peace with what she had decided to do. Now all that was left was to make it happen, but inside she was worried. Maybe that could be the last time she would see him, see any of them. If she got away, would they just leave Ross alone? Would they come for him? Try and find out what else he knew about her? On the other hand, he didn't know anything.

She'd been careful not to tell Ross any more than what he needed to know. Those things he'd been involved with had all been done through the laptop, through the computer system. She didn't know anybody better at covering that up than Ross.

Through the afternoon, Kirsten talked with Johann about his plans. His first thought was now to go to Finland and head up to the far north to hide out up there. Kirsten pointed out this was very different to South America and catching passage on a boat, but the man was worried about putting anyone else in jeopardy. Up there he could live out on his own. Up there it would be easy. Why would anyone look in Finland, that close to Russia? *He wouldn't sit that close to Russia surely,* thought Kirsten. The other end of the earth seemed the more sensible solution, but they would all know that and that's where they would look for him. She wasn't so sure it would work in that particular way.

'Do you have any money? Anything with which to start up there?' The man shook his head. 'Okay, then,' said Kirsten, 'we'll be able to get you something. I have stashed around here and there certain monies. It won't be much, but it'll get you through the first month. Finland is euros. You're lucky, I've got quite a few of those. If you'd been going somewhere more obscure, I probably wouldn't hold that type of currency.'

Kirsten gave him a smile, but Johann's face was full of worry.

'How do I get on a plane?' he said. 'How do I sneak on? It's not going to work now, is it? They've been looking for me everywhere. My picture, can you disguise me well enough? And if I'm at an airport, I'm just grabbed, that's it. Or do I take a boat? Who's going to take me on to Finland? Originally, I thought I could maybe get on a long-haul flight, but too much has happened now. Maybe I could drive, go down all the way through England and through the tunnel and make my way up from there, but they'll be watching at the borders.'

'We don't go that way,' said Kirsten. 'There are people who will do certain flights for you, flights they won't talk about to anyone. They're not always the nicest people to deal with, but they can be paid for the job. We just need someone to be able to get hold of them and organise it. We're not in the easiest place to be contacted at the moment, but luckily Alan Ross is, and he's not doing anything. He'll know how to organise it. He'll also know how to put a landing site together. One that's simple, but he's not daft.'

'But when would we go?' asked Johann.

'You go tonight. It's very short notice, but that's the point. That's what they're good at. They get you into the aircraft, take you up, drop you in Finland and they leave. It's usually a makeshift aircraft, short take-off and landing, but somewhere that can land, maybe on a road, not use a traditional airfield. That way nobody's prepared for it. Then when they get up, they keep low, very low. They fly maybe five hundred to a thousand feet all the way up over the sea, keep below any radars of air traffic. If we can do it without anyone noticing all the better, but even if we don't and they see you get on board, as long as they can get any sort of a start, they'll be good for it. I'll place a call to Ross, get it all set up for you.'

Johann didn't seem totally convinced, not that the man had much of an option. Kirsten placed a call from her mobile direct to the safe house where Ross was staying. At first, he sounded surprised. As Kirsten talked him through the procedures, who to go to and where to find out about them, Ross seemed more and more comfortable. She told him where in the house to find an account with which they could transfer money through as

181

well for the flight. Then she sat back and waited for him to organise what was going to happen.

It was around eight o'clock when the return phone call came back. Kirsten listened as Ross detailed that they'd be coming in a high winged aircraft, landing on a street. He said that it barely looked like a street, more of a back road through the fields. Just off of Four Penny. Kirsten didn't know the place, but when he said close to Embo and Dornoch, she knew where she was. She took down the coordinates and punched them into her map, looking into her phone's map function and realised they were actually quite far out.

She activated the satellite function and the street map view and wondered how on earth they could be accurate enough to land there, especially without any lights, but that was not her problem. Her problem was getting Johann to the plane and that would begin shortly. They would have to leave the compound, route round the fields to find a car. From there, they would pick up money from Kirsten's dumpsite and then head over towards Embo and Four Penny. From where they were, it was less than an hour away, but having seven hours yet to go, Kirsten decided she just wanted to hold up and wait.

Where they were was a good hiding place. It was unlikely anyone would find them. Once you put yourself back out there, it became much more difficult, and she wasn't operating on her own either. Johann Stein might have been a genius when it came to delivery systems for biochemical weapons, but he wasn't that good at staying hidden. He certainly didn't understand any spycraft.

At midnight, Kirsten gave the nod, saying they should make their move. She got past the cameras at the compound, and they walked through the fields back down to the hamlets she'd been in the previous night. From there, she stole a car, the same one, and they drove north before cutting through a country lane at the back of what looked like a broken-down hut. Kirsten pulled up a lid that had been grown over with grass. Sitting underneath was a large green canvas bag. She opened it, counted through the euros that were sitting in it and reckoned there must be the best part of three thousand euros. She took it, dropped it in the back of the car, and then simply sat, waiting.

The run for Four Penny would have to be done at pace, not out in the open for too long. She reckoned from where she was it was maybe a twenty-minute run. As they sat in the car, Johann suddenly put his hand across and took Kirsten's in his.

'I just want to say thank you. You could have taken me in,' he said. 'The thing is that most people wouldn't go out of their way, wouldn't believe, simply say I was overreacting, but I'm not with this. I know what it can do. It has to be put aside and I don't want to die. I did think about that. The easiest way to stop all this, just go and throw myself in front of a train. Then I thought I'll just not speak, but they have ways of making me speak, don't they? They can get things out of you.'

Kirsten knew that to be true, so she simply smiled back.

'Thank you,' he said. 'Whatever else happens now, thank you for taking a chance on me. What will your future be, though?' he said. 'You could come with me if you want.'

'No,' said Kirsten. 'Whatever my future will be, it won't be for that. I'm not going to spend my life on the run. They can come after me if they want. I'm hoping they just simply fire me, but they may turn around and try me for treason. But I'm not giving you to anybody else. I'm standing up for you. I don't know what that will mean, if it comes to a court.' Kirsten

183

began to laugh as if any of this would end up in a court.

'Well, thank you,' he said. 'Thank you from the bottom of my heart. It's hard going. Never again while I see Georgina. I had hopes once, hopes that I could steal Georgina away, but she's too wedded to her vows. It's not her husband. She doesn't like him, but she won't leave her family or kids. Said she has an obligation, but I don't see that. The man broke that, a cord that was between. I hope she's happy, but I guess I'll never know.'

'No, you won't,' said Kirsten. 'It's all we can hope for. If I have to run, I'll leave behind a brother, although he doesn't know me anymore.'

She sniffed back a tear, fought to maintain her focus. The car was dark as was the little path they were on. Only the occasional shadow from a half-lit moon gave her cause for concern.

'Are you sure they'll be able to land?' asked Johann. 'What do we do if it goes wrong, and they can't come here? The weather throws them off. Something like that or that they just betray us. What do we do?'

'We go back to the compound,' said Kirsten, 'we go back there. We stay there until we can work out the next plan. Get somebody else to take you, but these people, when they say they're going to be there, they'll be there. It's not an inconsiderate amount of money we're paying them, but don't expect the aircraft to be big. If it's a landing like that, I expect it's only going to be a two-person plane. The flight to Sweden could be long. They may land somewhere else first to fuel up, but whatever happens, Johann, good luck to you. Once you're in that plane, don't hesitate. Don't wait for me. I can get clear. I know how to handle myself.'

'I've seen that,' he said. 'I've seen that plenty.'

Kirsten looked out the window. The man was paying a compliment. She didn't want it. Since she'd come into the service, she'd been taught not only how to creep around, how to steal if necessary, how to coerce, but she was also taught how to kill. She remembered the first time, not far north of Inverness, protecting the couple in the camper van. She remembered shooting the man who was about to shoot the first minister. For all that she was doing her job, it still didn't feel right. It still felt that there should have been another way. There hadn't been. Too often it had been just there and then in the moment, someone else with a gun trained on you. Maybe out of this life was better.

Her thoughts turned to Craig. She couldn't even talk to him at the moment. Once Johann was away, she was breaking that rule. She'd find him, she'd speak to him and she'd work out where he stood.

That was the other thing that the service did to you. Everything now, she had to think of it from every angle. What was the agenda? Whose agenda was it? How were they playing this? Nothing was ever just simple anymore. Why did that woman order bacon and eggs that morning? Why was the man driving a Mondeo and not a different car? Everything was a calculation. Everything was being worked out in her head. What motives? Then she thought of Anna Hunt, and how she'd been dying at the caravan. Had she got away? Was she okay? Kirsten had worked well with the woman, but now she felt she was almost on the other side. Anna seemed as ruthless as anyone.

'It's time, Johann,' she said and started the car. As she reached the end of the road and turned to her right, she put the car lights on. After a couple of bends she realised they were picking lights up in the rear-view mirror. 'That's odd. Don't like that.'

'What's up?' asked Johann.

'Someone behind us. I think they might be on our tail.'

'How?' asked Johann. He looked at her and Kirsten saw the car behind her speed up. Suddenly, she was shunted, and she fought to contain the control of the car before putting her foot down on the accelerator.

'I'm afraid we've been spotted,' said Kristen. 'Hold on!'

Chapter 23

Kirsten put the pedal to the floor and raced along the road with two cars in pursuit. They were both significantly higher-powered cars, so instead of heading for the larger roads, Kirsten made sure she stayed to the small country back ones. Beside her, she could feel that Johann was becoming tense. He hung onto the handle above his door, and several times, she heard him swear in his native tongue.

Kirsten turned hard right, clipping the edge of a hedge, causing the wheel to bounce up, but the car managed to hold the corner and drove on. Meanwhile behind her, the pursuing car hit the corner and was then shoved on into the hedge by the car following behind. Kirsten barely saw what happened in her rear-view mirror, but it confirmed to her something. There wasn't just one party out here at the moment, there were at least two.

'Do you know where you're going?' said Johann desperately.

'Kind of,' said Kirsten. 'I know where we're meant to be. I know when we're meant to be there, and at the moment, we're heading in the opposite direction.'

'Why?'

'Because I can't arrive there early. Got to arrive there bang on time and get you into that plane and away.'

'What about you?' asked Johann.

'I'll get out of here. It's what I do, part of my job. Once you're on that plane, they won't see me for dust.'

Kirsten turned down another country lane and saw a car coming directly down the road at her. It didn't slow down, flash its lights or any other reasonable manoeuvre, so she assumed it was from one of the parties following them. There was an open gate about halfway along leading into a field, and she turned hard through the corner, praying that the field wasn't too mucky. There hadn't been a lot of rain recently, and the lack of it might just be enough so that the car didn't sink into the field.

As her headlights lit up the field in front of her, Kirsten sent up a word of thanks realising that it was grass, hard, and not a ploughed field. She turned in and saw others following in behind her. Driving over to one corner of the field, she spun the car around, rolled down the window, firing shots across the other cars. Her own window was then blown out, glass shattering, and she covered her face desperately, hoping Johann was doing the same. But Kirsten also went on the attack, driving into the back near side of one of the cars causing it to spin. Another car lurched past her by the nearest of margins. Kirsten was able to turn out past them and onto the road she'd previously come from. She took a left, heading along the country lane with the wind racing in through the missing windscreen.

'Take something and knock that glass all out,' she said. 'Don't need it coming off into our faces.' Kirsten had her hand up, protecting her eyes as Johann reached up, using the chamois he found in the door pocket of the car. The glass tinkled as it fell in, but the wind drowned the noise as Kirsten continued to go at a pace. Reaching the end of the lane, she took a left onto a more substantial road but was almost immediately picked up by at least three cars.

It's the back end of nowhere, thought Kirsten. *How do they know where we were? Was there some sort of satellite feed?'* Her mind raced towards Ross. Had they found him? Had they even tortured him for the information? Hopefully, he'd had the wit to stay to ground.

Kirsten reached another road, and, this time, turned onto what was a much more significant A-class road. There was a car coming the other way. As she got closer, it spun, coming to a halt, stopping across the road. There was a large ditch on the left-hand side. Kirsten threw her car over to the other side, rounding up onto some grass, catching a piece of fence at the front end, which took out the headlight. She managed to slide, however, off the bank and put the car back on the road. In the rear-view mirror, she saw these two cars follow until a third ploughed into the car that was sat straddled across the road. She was leaving a trail of carnage behind her, one that she wasn't comfortable with. One that she certainly wasn't responsible for causing.

'How far out are we?' shouted Johann.

'Five minutes. They should be here in five minutes. I'd like to do a circle around where they're going to land, but I don't want to give that position away too quick. I'm just praying that they've picked us up, and they don't actually know where the landing site is because if they do, we're snookered.'

Kirsten kept charging along, squinting with her eyes as the wind cut in through the absent window. Suddenly, Johann shouted at her and pointed up into the sky.

'There's something there. Something flying around.'

Kirsten glanced at her watch. *Were they early?* She tried to gauge whereabouts the plane was routing towards, but having to keep one eye on the road and one eye up in the air, it was hard to judge anything. She took a left off the main road, charging down now towards Dornoch, a town asleep at this hour of the morning. The road narrowed and she passed shops and houses she recognised before reaching the centre of the town, where she cut left towards Embo. She passed a set of holiday houses at breakneck speed, still with at least two to three cars on her. As she passed the turning for Embo, a motorcycle pulled out quickly, coming up towards her. He gained traction on her and got up alongside on the passenger side of the car, and Johann covered his head, crouching down, desperately afraid.

'Just open the door,' shouted Kirsten at him. 'Open the door.'

The motorcycle was now up and adjacent to the passenger door. A gun had been taken out. Kirsten, seeing Johann had frozen, threw herself past him, pushing open the door, causing the motorcyclist to spin off and crash into a number of trees. However, her own car then slid sideways, and she fought to get it back on the road. Somewhere, the tire hit something, and she heard it explode as she fought to maintain her track.

'Get with it. You're going to be on the run in a second. Stay with me.'

Her hand reached out and gave Johann a shove, but his face was pure white in terror. The car was starting to slow as well, and Kirsten was struggling to find speed. As she went past Embo and further north, she knew the turn for the landing road was coming. As she got closer, she saw a number of headlights further north but heading south. Everyone was converging. Meanwhile, above her, she could see the plane coming into land, almost flying at an impossibly slow speed.

At the last second, Kirsten realised she was approaching the corner too fast. She tried to slow, but she'd no traction due to the wheel that had been shot out. The car turned and spun over once before landing on its base again.

For a moment, she was shaking. Kirsten then grabbed her gun from inside her jacket, opened the door, and shouted at Johann to get running. In front of them was a small country lane with an aircraft landing on it. The aircraft looked impossibly small, maybe with one person inside, two at the most.

'Go,' shouted Kirsten at Johann. She took up a position behind the car and began firing at those following her. 'Just go,' she shouted.

She watched Johann begin to run, the plane further down the small road, now having successfully landed. A couple of cars came towards the turn too quickly as well, and Kirsten tore off to the lane. Two cars slid into her own car, sitting on the corner, causing one to flip over. Kirsten fired back at where the accident had happened, trying to deter anyone from following them down the lane, and then, she turned and ran, desperate to catch up with Johann.

As he got closer to the plane, which was still a quarter of a mile up the road, Kirsten saw somebody coming out of the bushes. She was unsure who they were, what side they were on, but whatever was happening, they were making a beeline for Johann. She watched him take out the gun she'd given him, but he was incapable of firing it, almost like he didn't know what to do.

191

Fortunately, the other side weren't interested in killing him. Instead, they seemed to be looking to make a capture. Kirsten dropped to one knee, her gun in front of her and fired off a round. She saw the first man coming towards Johann bend down as if hit, and she was back up on her feet, running towards him again. She saw Johann lash out with a punch, which momentarily stunned the man on the floor, but his colleague behind him, ran forward, grabbing Johann.

Kirsten was now less than twenty metres away, and she fired at the man on the ground, causing him to topple over. The second man she couldn't shoot, as he was engaged with Johann, so Kirsten holstered her pistol and made a flying tackle on Johann's assailant, along with Johann, all three toppling to the ground, but the assailant was quick.

Rolling back up, Kirsten got to her feet as well and ducked to one side as the man threw a punch at her. She unleashed a kick from behind, driving the ball of her foot up and into the man's temple, causing him to spin off to the ground. As he went to stand up, she struck him on the back of the head with the butt of her gun. She watched as he tumbled to the ground.

Turning to look back up at the entrance of the country lane, Kirsten could see a car starting to come through, and she dropped to her knee, firing.

'Keep running,' she shouted to Johann. 'Just keep going.' There was less than maybe fifty yards to go now. If she could hold the car off, he'd be safe.

Kirsten tried to aim at the tyres, first one shot, then another. Then she put two towards the windscreen. Another shot must have done something when she heard a bang, and the car rather disappointingly simply turned right and crashed into a small fence post. Kirsten looked behind her. Johann was nearly there.

Out of the car came five men firing at her, and Kirsten dived off the road behind a small hedge. From there, she started taking pot shots, but she watched as half of the crew raced around the field and not up the road. She saw one man fall that she shot at before a bullet zipped over her head. She turned and started running up the hedge row, letting herself go up another twenty yards before turning back to fire again. By now, Johann was reaching the plane.

Three men were running on the other side of the road through the field, but she watched as one ran past her. She took a shot, but she couldn't get him. She went to shoot, finding it hard to pick him out in the dark, but then something caught her shoulder. It was a nick, a close gunshot, but it did make her fall over to the ground. From there, she struggled to get back up in that moment, and she knew that they'd be past her. Rising up, she saw a man on the road who presumably had shot at her, and Kirsten fired back, taking three shots before the man fell over. She turned to see three men at the plane, one with his hand around Johann, dragging him back and away from it.

'No,' shouted Kirsten, hurdling back over the hedge and now running for the plane. One man turned to shoot at her, but she was quicker, and he fell to the floor. The other men were too close to Johann, and she couldn't do anything about that. One turned and Kirsten got up close, grabbing him, throwing him off Johann. The second, however, stuck a knife into Kirsten's shoulder, and she yelled, grabbing it, and pulling it out.

The first man she'd thrown off was now behind her, drilling punches into her ribs before throwing her off to one side. Kirsten's body was screaming in agony, and she was lying on the ground next to the hedgerow when she looked up at the small plane. It was as promised, high wings and a high tail, and it landed rather incredibly, but then, she looked and saw the pilot. He was an older-looking man and was currently wearing a large grey coat.

As she lay there struggling to get back to her feet, she saw Johann being dragged away by the two men, and the man in the grey coat stepped out to follow them. As he came into the beam given by the anti-collision light on the tail of the aircraft, Kirsten could see Godfrey. He was raising his gun.

'No,' she shouted. 'No.'

Johann was getting dragged away. Johann was going to become Russia's. Godfrey raised his gun and simply fired two shots. Kirsten could see the Russians react, first looking at themselves, then realising that the man they were carrying had become an even heavier weight. They started dragging him. His feet had gone limp, and then they realised Johann Stein was dead.

'No,' shouted Kirsten. 'No.'

The two men holding Johann Stein dropped him and ran. They were on foreign soil. The prize they had come for was no longer there. They had to get out.

Kirsten hauled herself back to her feet, struggled over towards the aircraft, where Godfrey looked at her with an air of disgust. Kirsten raised her gun, pointing it at him.

'Why?' she said. 'Why? We could have him gotten away. He could have been all right.'

'You know why,' said Godfrey. 'We all know why, but some of us can follow our orders. Others seem to get a little too emotional.'

Kirsten held her gun up, now less than five metres from

Godfrey. With a single pull of the trigger, she could blow him away, and she felt he deserved it. The man had just killed someone doing the right thing, someone who was trying to protect everyone. If she did it now, who would know it was her and not the Russians?

'If you don't mind, I'm going to start clearing up now.'

'I'll kill you,' shouted Kirsten.

'No, you won't. When you came, I said to Anna Hunt, "She has a flaw." You won't kill me. Of that, I'm pretty sure.' Godfrey turned and made his way back inside the small aircraft.

Kirsten could feel the tears streaming down her face. There was a cry from back down the road, but the aircraft, with an engine still running, pulled away down the road and then got airborne incredibly quickly before lifting up into the night sky. Kirsten looked over and saw Johann Stein's face, impassive. It seemed the hunt was over. There was nothing left to do.

She turned, climbed over the hedge into the field, and started to run as hard as she could away from the scene. In her mind, the everyday basics were screaming at her. *Where's my shelter? Where do I lie low? I've got an injury. Where do I get treatment?*

Above that, questions about whether Ross was safe raced through her head. *What would Godfrey do to those who had assisted her? What would he do to her?* And yet, on top of all that cake was a layer that said, *I failed him. I just failed him.*

Chapter 24

Kirsten watched the coffee, the steam rising from it, and deliberately held back from tasting it. She wanted him to take that first sip with her and he was unfashionably late. Normally she had to watch her timings because he would be there at least on the dot if not before, but maybe he had been detained. As she sat staring at the coffee, she heard a voice behind her.

'Sorry, they tried to get me to go into a press conference. Hope's covering it—told her I had something important to do.'

'Not for a murder investigation,' said Kirsten; 'you didn't just shirk a murder investigation conference.'

'No,' said Macleod, 'something about modern policing. Chief Inspector wanted me on the panel. Can you imagine? Who in their right mind? Soon as I told him Hope was available, he seemed to get much more excited.'

'A couple of hours with you or a couple of hours with Hope? Can't imagine what got him excited.' Kirsten watched as Macleod took off a long grey coat and put it over the chair opposite Kirsten.

He pulled it out and sat down. 'I see you've already ordered,' he said.

'Well, I didn't want to hang around. I'm still not the flavour of the month.'

'Of course not,' said Macleod. 'I'm just amazed you're still here.'

'Well, I think Godfrey wants rid of me. He could come after me, put me down, but I think he's scared.'

'I've never met the man,' said Macleod, 'but these secret service types, they don't tend to be scared of people.'

'No, they're not. But I have things on Godfrey. I'm not even sure that's his real name.'

There was a voice behind her. Kirsten almost jumped when it said, 'It's one of many he's got.'

Macleod stood up from his chair and Kirsten saw him put out a hand. A female hand took it, shook it and then sat down in the seat between Macleod and Kirsten. She had an arm wrapped up in a sling and was wearing a smart jacket, but only one arm was through. She had jeans underneath the jacket, which was highly unusual. One foot had a large cast on it. On Anna Hunt's face was a mix of scars and bruises.

'You don't mind if I butt in, do you?' said Anna. 'I just felt that maybe some things needed to be said.'

'Actually, it was a private conversation,' said Kirsten, but she thought Anna Hunt was going to become thunderous because her face turned red.

'I took you on board, you became one of us, and then you betrayed us like that?'

'I don't think we should get into what you were actually doing.' said Macleod, but Kirsten put her hand up.

'It's all right, Seoras, I'm a big girl now. I can handle myself. You gave me orders that were impossible to follow, Anna. You left me out in the dark. You didn't confide in me, didn't turn around and discuss. You lied to me about what the man was actually doing. You made it out he was a traitor, had to be brought in or killed, when, in fact, it's you guys that are betraying us, our country, everything about it.'

'I wonder if you wouldn't mind getting me a coffee,' said Anna to Macleod; 'it's just I feel that we may have something to discuss here and a couple of minutes on our own wouldn't go amiss.'

Macleod looked over at Kirsten who simply gave him a nod. 'As you will,' said Macleod, and he walked off inside to the coffee house, leaving the two women at the outside table.

'You shouldn't indulge him,' said Anna.

'And you shouldn't leave your people out in the dark. If it wasn't for him, I'd probably be dead. You don't go near my friends.'

'Near your friends,' said Anna. 'Who are you giving orders to? Remember who you work for.'

'Work for you? Do I still? I don't think Godfrey's going to have me near him again.'

'No, he won't, and you'll not come back to the service, but sometimes the service comes back to you, so don't disappear too far. It's my fault, really,' said Anna. 'Godfrey warned me; he said to me, "She's not got it."'

'Not got what?' asked Kirsten. 'Not got the ability to make a decision? Not got the ability to follow orders?'

'No,' said Anna, 'not got the ability to switch off her moral compass. Not got the ability to turn around and make the decision that you don't want to make. I didn't tell you what he was doing because I knew fine rightly it was not something you could deal with. You still struggle when you kill people. Not physically. Physically, you can take out most people; mentally, it still gets to you, doesn't it? The turmoil is still there. It gets to us all in some ways, but not like with you. You can't switch the conscience off. You actually wonder could you have done better when somebody was trying to blow your head off. It might be laudable. Might even be something worth writing about, but in a service agent, it really doesn't work.

'Then you decide what's best for the country, you make the decision. You were going to let that man run around this world where he could be picked up by anybody else and we would be under threat.'

'Or I could have taken him to you, where you were going to use that very weapon he concocted, to push around other nations, to get what we want.'

'Dog-eat-dog world out there,' said Anna Hunt, 'I'm afraid you'll find.'

'How did he turn up in the aircraft? I take it you got to Ross.'

'We got to Ross; it took time, but we did. He wasn't easy to break.'

'If you've hurt him, I will come for you,' said Kirsten.

'We didn't have to do much. He spoke, but it did make us struggle to get there in time. Not a daft cookie at all.'

Kirsten sat back in her chair, sweat pouring off her now. 'Don't ever come after them,' she said, 'none of them. They're good people doing good jobs. They don't need you or me or what we do to get involved.'

'Of course not,' said Anna. 'This is goodbye. Like I said, the service doesn't want you, but beware. The service changes its mind. I'll be seeing you.' The woman walked off just as Macleod was coming back.

'Hey,' he shouted. 'Do you not want your coffee?'

'Don't really drink it,' said Anna and left Macleod shaking his head. He put the coffee down on the table and joined Kirsten.

'What was that about?'

'If I told you, I'd have to kill you,' said Kirsten and gave a little chuckle.

'Seriously,' said Macleod, 'what was it about?'

'The ground rules. I'm not to talk about them. They don't talk to anybody that I know, either. It's a parting of the ways, Seoras. I'm out and free. Only cost Johann Stein's life.'

'That wasn't your fault,' said Macleod. 'You can't blame yourself for that.'

'But I do. As you do, when you get things wrong; just the jobs we work in, isn't it?'

'Where are you going?' asked Macleod.

'I don't know,' said Kirsten. 'Somewhere away for a bit. Somewhere where I can work out what happens next. It had all gone so well. I had a team and that team got shot up, and then I find out about the side of the service that I don't like. Didn't you think it would come to this?'

'I'd hoped for better,' said Macleod. 'I'd hoped you'd manage to convince them or change them in some way, but I don't know them. I just knew if I got good people in there, that maybe better things would happen.' Kirsten took her coffee and drunk it, looking over at Macleod.

'Ross will be back at work next week. He's okay.'

'I know he's okay,' said Macleod. 'He was always fine. Can handle himself, that boy. He's not just someone who can operate behind a computer, he holds my team together. All of it. He says it's so that the man with the brain can do the thinking. I think the man with the brain's getting too old,' Macleod laughed.

'You can't,' said Kirsten.

'Can't what? Retire? Why can't I retire? You've just run off. You've just called it quits. You're not even forty. In fact, you're not even thirty, are you?'

'I haven't called it quits, Seoras. Just need to know what to do.'

'You can always come back. Police can always do with someone like you.'

Kirsten shook her head. 'No. I've been outside of the rulebook. It might be a lot harder to come back in. Can't just punch somebody when they get on your nerves.'

'Well, you can't get caught doing it,' said Macleod. 'That's quite important these days. Changed all around. Keep yourself on our books, though. Keep in touch,' said Macleod. 'Something comes up, I'll give you a shout. You never know. That's the thing. There's always something bad happening. We have a murder. We have bombers, gun plots, terrorists, or even people who are just dumb enough to create something that can wipe out a nation in three days.'

'I never told you that,' said Kirsten. 'Never in that detail.'

'No,' said Macleod. 'You didn't. Ross trusts me a lot more than you do. Ross told me everything and I told him I couldn't get involved. Then you pitched up. That's when I knew you were struggling.'

'I'm sorry I got you all involved. Still, maybe it's for the best.'

'If it keeps that Anna Hunt woman off my back, it's always for the best. She took over that scene in the shopping centre and it got at me. She took bodies away, bodies that should've been held accountable. It's not right,' said Macleod. 'What they were doing, the way they went after him, it wasn't right.'

'You'll never get them, though. You can't investigate that way. Official secrets and all that.'

'No,' said Macleod. 'I won't and I know my limits and I know when to stop, and maybe you've learnt to as well. Go and take some time. See what else you want from your career.'

Kirsten stood up and drained her coffee and walked round the table, crouched down, and put her arms around Macleod. She gave him a kiss on the cheek and held him tight again.

'I'm not going to look at the career,' she said. 'What career will come, will come. Wasn't that long ago, I lost my family. My brother went into care, but I found three others. Then I lost them, and I went into the service, and in that service, I found some friends and we nearly lost them completely. I certainly have lost them now. I'm going off to see about family. See if I find a new one.'

Kirsten put her arm up, giving a wave across the road and she stood up beside Macleod almost waiting. He stood up, joining her and she reached down and took his hand in hers. A silver car pulled up and a man got out of the rear of it, looking tall and immaculate in a suit. 'Seoras, this is Craig. He's just walked away from the service for me because he said I mean more to him than it does to him. If this doesn't work out, will you give him a job?'

Macleod laughed. 'No, but he's a lucky man.' Macleod stepped forward putting a hand out and shaking Craig's.

Kirsten turned back to Macleod again. 'I've got to go,' she said, and the tears started to stream down her eyes. She looked up at Macleod, but his face had that same coldness to it she'd always known, as if he was processing things in the background. Then he reached forward and gave her a kiss on the forehead.

'Don't go too far,' he said. 'Keep in touch. You never know what's around the corner.'

Kirsten watched Craig get back inside the car, got to the door herself, climbed in and shut it. She rolled down the window. 'Tell Alan I owe him. I hope he's very happy.'

'Let's do this again,' said Macleod, and sat back down, taking his coffee in his hand. He watched as the car drove away and then sat back taking in the Inverness street. More cars passed this way and that, and he finished the coffee he was drinking and put it down. Beside his own cup was the one he brought out for Anna Hunt.

'Yes, the Chief Inspector can wait a while longer,' he said, and picked up the second cup.

Read on to discover the Patrick Smythe series!

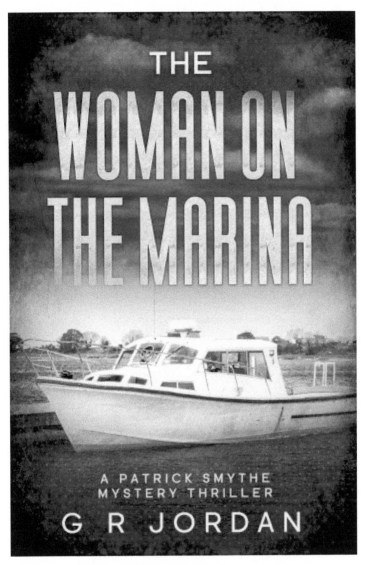

THE

WOMAN ON
THE MARINA

A PATRICK SMYTHE
MYSTERY THRILLER

G R JORDAN

Start your Patrick Smythe journey here!

Patrick Smythe is a former Northern Irish policeman who

after suffering an amputation after a bomb blast, takes to the sea between the west coast of Scotland and his homeland to ply his trade as a private investigator. Join Paddy as he tries to work to his own ethics while knowing how to bend the rules he once enforced. Working from his beloved motorboat 'Craigantlet', Paddy decides to rescue a drug mule in this short story from the pen of G R Jordan.

Join G R Jordan's monthly newsletter about forthcoming releases and special writings for his tribe of avid readers and then receive your free Patrick Smythe short story.

Go to https://bit.ly/PatrickSmythe for your Patrick Smythe journey to start!

About the Author

GR Jordan is a self-published author who finally decided at forty that in order to have an enjoyable lifestyle, his creative beast within would have to be unleashed. His books mirror that conflict in life where acts of decency contend with self-promotion, goodness stares in horror at evil, and kindness blindsides us when we at our worst. Corrupting our world with his parade of wondrous and horrific characters, he highlights everyday tensions with fresh eyes whilst taking his methodical, intelligent mainstays on a roller-coaster ride of dilemmas, all the while suffering the banter of their provocative sidekicks.

A graduate of Loughborough University where he masqueraded as a chemical engineer but ultimately played American football, Gary had worked at changing the shape of cereal flakes and pulled a pallet truck for a living. Watching vegetables freeze at -40'C was another career highlight and he was also one of the Scottish Highlands "blind" air traffic controllers.

These days he has graduated to answering a telephone to people in trouble before telephoning other people to sort it out.

Having flirted with most places in the UK, he is now based in the Isle of Lewis in Scotland where his free time is spent between raising a young family with his wife, writing, figuring out how to work a loom and caring for a small flock of chickens. Luckily, his writing is influenced by his varied work and life experience as the chickens have not been the poetical inspiration he had hoped for!

You can connect with me on:

🌐 https://grjordan.com

📱 https://facebook.com/carpetlessleprechaun

Subscribe to my newsletter:

✉ https://bit.ly/PatrickSmythe

Also by G R Jordan

G R Jordan writes across multiple genres including crime, dark and action adventure fantasy, feel good fantasy, mystery thriller and horror fantasy. Below is a selection of his work. Whilst all books are available across online stores, signed copies are available at his personal shop.

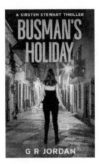

Busman's Holiday (Kirsten Stewart Thrillers #8)
https://grjordan.com/product/busmans-holiday
Kirsten seeks romance and sun on leaving the service. A chance encounter leaves her partner in the middle of a kidnapping. Can Kirsten find her beloved before a terrorist executes him in the name of freedom?

When Kirsten and Craig take a sun drenched holiday in an attempt to cement their love, little do they suspect their quaint destination will become part of a country's nightmare. The black hand rises, murdering a local mayor, and takes Craig hostage, forcing Kirsten to become a merciless rescuer once again. With no back-up, in a land she doesn't understand, the Service's black sheep must curry favours and avoid the local police as she brings down a country's dark underbelly.

How dark your passions when your soul is uneasy!

Anti-social Behaviour (A Highlands & Islands Detective Thriller #20)
https://grjordan.com/product/antisocial-behaviour
A youth is found dead at a children's playpark. A stolen car burnt out with the joyriders inside. Can Macleod discover the avenging angel brutally restoring the highland's peace and quiet?

When a spate of deaths indicating teenagers as targets sends Macleod and McGrath into a very public hunt for killer, they must walk in view of the hottest debate of the day. But when Hope believes she sees an angle that points the blame at those who responsible for the nation's safety, Macleod must trust his Sergeant's instincts while dodging a career ending bullet.

It was all easier back in the day, or was it?

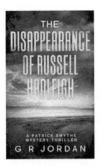

The Disappearance of Russell Hadleigh (Patrick Smythe Book 1)

https://grjordan.com/product/the-disappearance-of-russell-hadleigh

A retired judge fails to meet his golf partner. His wife calls for help while running a fantasy play ring. When Russians start co-opting into a fairly-traded clothing brand, can Paddy untangle the strands before the bodies start littering the golf course?

In his first full novel, Patrick Smythe, the single-armed former policeman, must infiltrate the golfing social scene to discover the fate of his client's husband. Assisted by a young starlet of the greens, Paddy tries to understand just who bears a grudge and who likes to play in the rough, culminating in a high stakes showdown where lives are hanging by the reaction of a moment. If you love pacey action, suspicious motives and devious characters, then Paddy Smythe operates amongst your kind of people.

Love is a matter of taste but money always demands more of its suitor.

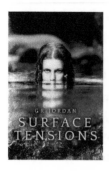

Surface Tensions (Island Adventures Book 1)
https://grjordan.com/product/surface-tensions
Mermaids sighted near a Scottish island. A town exploding in anger and distrust. And Donald's got to get the sexiest fish in town, back in the water.

"Surface Tensions" is the first story in a series of Island adventures from the pen of G R Jordan. If you love comic moments, cosy adventures and light fantasy action, then you'll love these tales with a twist. Get the book that amazon readers said, "perfectly captures life in the Scottish Hebrides" and that explores "human nature at its best and worst".

Something's stirring the water!

Corpse Reviver (A Contessa Munroe Mystery #1)
https://grjordan.com/product/corspe-reviver

A widowed Contessa flees to the north-ern waters in search of adventure. An entrepreneur dies on an ice pack excursion. But when the victim starts moonlighting from his locked cabin, can the Contessa uncover the true mystery of his death?

Catriona Cullodena Munroe, widow of the late Count de Los Palermo, has fled the family home, avoiding the scramble for title and land. As she searches for the life she always wanted, the Contessa, in the company of the autistic and rejected Tiff, must solve the mystery of a man who just won't let his business go.

Corpse Reviver is the first murder mystery involving the formidable and sometimes downright rude lady of leisure and her straight talking niece. Bonded by blood, and thrown together by fate, join this pair of thrill seekers as they realise that flirting with danger brings a price to pay.